A look Beth couldn't read crossed Lori's face as she nodded. "Yes, that's very strange."

Then she asked, "What else, Beth? Surely there was more happening than just two births."

"Yes, there was. I didn't know about it that night, but a freeway pileup brought so many injured into the hospital that every available doctor and nurse was called in to take care of them. The woman who died giving birth had been in the accident, too. I guess she was in pretty bad shape." Beth gave a laugh without amusement. "I picked a bad time to have a baby."

"You certainly did." Lori looked away.

Beth looked down at Stevie trying to go back to sleep. She tried to smile and found that she couldn't. A tear slid from her eye. Without taking her gaze from the child she loved more than her own life, she spoke. "She isn't mine, is she?"

Lori's voice sounded as if it came from far away. "She's yours, Beth. You've had her all her life."

"Yes, but she isn't the baby I gave birth to." Beth's breath caught in her throat as she choked out. "Lori, where is my baby?"

MILDRED COLVIN is a native Missourian with three children, one son-in-law, and two grandchildren. She and her husband spent most of their married life providing a home for foster children but now enjoy baby-sitting the grandchildren. Mildred writes inspirational romance because in them the truth of God's presence, even in the midst of trouble, can be portrayed. Her desire is to continue writing stories that uplift and encourage.

Books by Mildred Colvin

HEARTSONG PRESENTS
HP435—Circle of Vengeance – as M.J. Conner
HP543—Cora
HP591—Eliza

This Child Is Mine

Mildred Colvin

Heartsong Presents

A note from the Author:
I love to hear from my readers! You may correspond
with me by writing:

Mildred Colvin
Author Relations
PO Box 719
Uhrichsville, OH 44683

ISBN 1-59310-521-5

THIS CHILD IS MINE

*Our mission is to publish and distribute inspirational products offer-
ing exceptional value and biblical encouragement to the masses.*

All scripture quotations are taken from the New King James
Version. Copyright © 1979, 1980, 1982 by Thomas Nelson, Inc.
Used by permission. All rights reserved.

PRINTED IN THE U.S.A.

Or check out our Web site at www.heartsongpresents.com

one

"Mo' wa-wa."

"More water?" Beth laughed and hugged her tiny daughter before lifting her high and swinging her around in a circle. "You can have all the water you want, sweetheart."

Yesterday she wouldn't have been so eager to hand over yet another sippy cup. But yesterday she had feared her daughter's frequent requests for water were a sign that she had inherited more from her father than his brown eyes. Now she knew better. She filled a sippy and added a couple of ice cubes before setting the baby down and handing her the cup.

While Stevie drank her water, Beth picked up the paper from the hospital lab to reaffirm what she already knew. Never had the word *negative* looked so wonderful. She skimmed the paper as she thought of Steven and the heartbreak of his last few months while diabetes took his health, then finally his life. Even as tears filled her eyes, her heart lifted in thanksgiving to God that Stevie did not have diabetes.

Beth's gaze rested on what should have been an insignificant space on the form. Blood type—AB-positive. She frowned. The lab had made a mistake. Stevie had O-positive type blood. The form from the hospital where she was born clearly said *O*. Beth remembered. Besides, she couldn't have anything other than an O-positive blood type because Beth and Steven were both O-positive.

Air rushed from her lungs as she dropped into a chair and stared at the paper. How could the hospital have made such a mistake? She checked the name at the top to be sure it said Stevie Elizabeth Carter. It did. But if the blood type was

5

wrong, didn't that mean they had somehow mixed up Stevie's blood work with someone else's? And that meant she could still be diabetic.

Fear crept into Beth's heart as she looked at her precious daughter now playing with her favorite doll, the sippy cup forgotten on the floor beside her. At eighteen months, Stevie looked so much like Steven with her blond hair and large brown eyes. Did she have to have the sickness that killed him, too?

Beth glanced at the clock. A quarter to seven. Her first drop-off would arrive any minute. If she called now, she might catch Lori at home before she left for the hospital. She reached for the cordless phone and punched in her best friend's number.

Three rings later, Lori answered.

"Lori, just how accurate is that lab test?" Beth asked without preamble.

"Accurate? As in, is Stevie really free of diabetes?"

"No, I mean could they have gotten the blood work mixed up?"

"Beth!" Beth could imagine the disbelief on Lori's face. But Lori worked at the hospital. In the lab. She hadn't worked the day Stevie's test was done, but she knew the procedure and her coworkers. Of course she would think they were infallible. Her next words confirmed Beth's thought. "Of course not. What are you thinking? That there's something wrong with the test?"

Beth heard a car pull into her driveway and knew that Jack Helm, a three-year-old bombshell, was about to be dropped off at her door. Within five minutes, her home would become a day care—just as it did every weekday.

"There has to be, Lori. This paper says Stevie's blood type is AB-positive, but Steven's was O-positive just like mine. There was a paper when I brought Stevie home from the hospital that said Stevie has O-type blood."

Beth's doorbell rang. "Look, I've got to go. I want to talk to you tonight, though."

"All right, Beth," Lori said. "I'll come by after work, but I don't think it's possible that they could have made a mistake."

Beth had Jack settled for the moment with a bowl of oatmeal and a cup of orange juice when the doorbell rang again, and her second child arrived ready for her breakfast. By nine fifteen that morning, eight children ranging from a three-month-old baby to a four-year-old girl filled her living room with hopping, toddling, and crawling as they explored toys that never seemed to grow old until one noticed a different toy in another child's hand.

While the baby napped and the two eighteen-month-olds played nearby, Beth got out crayons, scissors, and paper for a short preschool session with her two-, three-, and four-year-olds.

The day went quickly through lunch and afternoon naps while Beth stayed too busy to spend much time thinking about her own problems. But as closing time neared and only two more children remained to be picked up, her mind went back to Steven and their precious baby.

Steven and Beth were sweethearts in high school. As Steven's fight against diabetes grew and they realized a pancreas transplant might not show up in time, Beth told him she'd rather live for a short time as a pauper with him than for a long time in wealth with any other man. So they married as soon as they graduated from college and lived mostly on her income from teaching preschool at Rainbow's End Day Care in Springfield for three and a half wonderful years.

Then Steven died, and Beth discovered she was carrying his child. She resigned her position with Rainbow's End and moved in with her parents in Blue Springs near Kansas City.

Beth's doorbell rang as her last pickup of the day arrived,

interrupting her thoughts. The door opened to Debbie's cries of "Mommy," and Beth stepped back while the little girl launched herself into her mother's arms.

Carolyn Hoover hugged her daughter and laughed. "She isn't glad to see me, is she?"

Beth smiled and shook her head. "Not that I can tell."

"And how's my boy?" Carolyn set her daughter down so she could lift her three-month-old son from the playpen where he slept. "How he sleeps through all Debbie's racket, I'll never understand."

"They get used to the noise, so it doesn't bother them," Beth answered as Stevie left her toy and crossed the room to stand close beside her. She smoothed her daughter's silky blond hair, loving the feel of her little body pressed against her leg.

She glanced out the front window and saw Lori's car pull into the driveway. Anxious to show her friend what she had discovered on Stevie's lab work, Beth set the diaper bag out.

"Debbie, would you like for me to help you with your coat?"

"No. Want Mommy." Debbie's lower lip stuck out and Beth sighed. Debbie seemed perfectly content all day long, but as soon as her mother showed up, she wanted nothing more to do with Beth. Normally, Beth didn't mind, but today she wanted to hurry the trio from her house so she could concentrate on her own problems.

Carolyn handed her sleeping son to Beth and took the coat. "Mrs. Carter does nice things for you all day, Debbie. You mustn't act naughty just because Mommy's here. The quicker you get your coat on, the quicker we can go home and eat."

Debbie shoved her arm through the coat sleeve. "Fries."

Carolyn laughed as she cast a sheepish look at Beth. "Now you know my secret for quick meals."

Beth smiled. "Don't feel bad. I've been guilty, too, when I'm so tired all I want to do is crash in front of the TV."

Just as Beth despaired of them ever leaving, Lori rang her doorbell and stuck her head around the door. "Hi. I was going to wait outside until you were finished in here, but I got cold sitting in the car."

Carolyn picked up the diaper bag and her daughter. She flashed a smile at Lori. "I'm on my way out now."

"Oh, I'm sorry. I didn't mean to rush you," Lori said.

Carolyn laughed. "No problem. We have to go find some french fries on our way home, anyway."

Beth stood with the baby now wrapped securely in a blanket. She gave a tiny shake of her head as an apology to Lori and said, "I'll help Carolyn out and be right back. Make yourself at home. Maybe Stevie can show you her new book."

"Hey, Stevie, have you got a new book?"

Beth heard Stevie's excited chatter as she followed Carolyn outside and knew Lori would be well entertained. As soon as Carolyn secured Debbie in her car seat, Beth handed the baby to her, told them good-bye, and ran for the house through a stiff February breeze.

"I wouldn't be surprised if it snowed tonight." Beth pushed the door closed, glad for the warmth of her little house.

Lori looked up from the book she and Stevie were reading. "We were so busy at the hospital today that I haven't paid much attention to the weather. Typical for this time of year, though. I think everyone and his brother has the flu."

"Yuck." Beth shivered. "I hope it isn't that bad, although I did have one gone today. Maybe he's down with the flu."

Lori nodded. "I wouldn't be surprised." She hugged Stevie. "Can you read that book by yourself while Mommy and I talk? Then when we're done, I'll treat you both to supper."

"No." Stevie shook her head and held the book toward Lori. "Wead."

Beth smiled at her stubborn daughter. From experience, she

knew bribery would not work. When Stevie wanted something, she went after it with the tenacity of a bulldog. That was one thing she had not inherited from her father. Steven had been easygoing.

The familiar ache settled in her chest as she thought of her husband, kind and generous to a fault. Stevie might have his coloring and she might have his long, delicate fingers, but this dogged determination to have her own way must have been a throwback to an earlier generation.

Lori and Stevie's continued argument caught Beth's attention.

"How about fries? Do you like them?" Lori asked the little girl. "I think your little friend was going to get some fries."

Stevie nodded and held the book out. "Wead."

Lori laughed, and Stevie giggled, her one dimple flashing.

"No, you read the book all by yourself, and I'll get you some fries."

Stevie stood on the sofa and turned to plop into Lori's lap, the book clutched securely in her small hands. She turned with a grin and pushed the book toward Lori. "Wead."

Beth laughed. "I think you've just lost, Lori. You may as well finish the book, then I'll show you the paper from the hospital."

Lori shook her head in mock indignation. "I'll read the book, then I'll still have to buy her fries."

"Fwies." Stevie mimicked Lori, making the women laugh.

"All right, I give." Lori shook her head and opened the book. *The Puppy Who Wanted a Home.*

Ten minutes later, Beth had her home back in order after the invasion of her busy day-care children. Stevie, tired of reading, jumped from Lori's lap to pull out a jack-in-the-box that Beth had just put away. Beth grabbed the opportunity to get the lab report and hand it to Lori.

"See, it says that Stevie tested negative for diabetes, but it has the wrong blood type. Here." She handed Lori another paper. "This is what the hospital in Kansas City gave me when Stevie was born. Look at the blood type on it. They're not the same, Lori. I'm afraid they used someone else's blood."

Lori looked from one paper to the other, a puzzled frown on her face. She shook her head. "That means we still don't know for sure if Stevie is in the clear."

"What can I do?" Beth felt frustrated from the emotional hills and valleys she had been forced to ride the last several years. She knew God had never promised an easy life, only that He would be with her. And He had been. Steven's sickness. Giving up her dream of teaching. Their marriage. His death. Stevie's birth. Starting and running her own business. God had been beside her through it all. He would not leave her alone. Peace washed through her heart and calmed her.

Beth looked at Lori and asked, "Can you do a blood test now?"

Lori's eyebrows shot up. "Tonight? Unofficial?"

Beth nodded. "Yes. Tonight. Lori, I know the hospitals are trustworthy. They probably seldom make a mistake. But you can't argue with me that a mistake hasn't been made." She tapped the two papers still clutched in Lori's hands. "Right here is proof. A child can't have two different blood types, now can she?"

"No." Lori shook her head. "That she cannot do."

Beth knew she was begging, but that was the least that she would do for Stevie. "Can you do it, Lori? Can you give a blood test?"

Lori frowned. "I shouldn't, but I will. Let's go get something to eat first, then go to the lab. You'd better hope no one decided to work late tonight and, for the record, Beth, I never did it."

"Don't worry. It's just for my peace of mind. I won't tell." Beth breathed easier knowing Lori would take care of things.

❧

A few snowflakes drifted in front of the headlights as Lori stopped first to get a hamburger and fries for Stevie. Beth and Lori each bought a chicken meal. Beth forced hers down as she watched Stevie and Lori eat.

Stevie remained quiet on the short drive to the hospital. When Lori parked the car, Beth lifted her sleeping baby from her car seat and together they went inside.

Recognizing the friend she had in Lori, Beth breathed a prayer of thanksgiving for Lori and her willingness to help. She wondered what she would have done after Steven's death without Lori and others from her church family. Although her parents had begged her to remain in Blue Springs with them after Stevie's birth, Beth preferred the independence that the move back to Bolivar had given her. A year later, when her father's job unexpectedly transferred him to Michigan, Beth was glad for her decision.

Opening a day care had been a challenge from the start but was worth all the headache of finding a suitable house and getting it approved by the state's health department. Although operating a day care was not her first choice of employment, she could think of nothing else in her line of work that would allow her to stay home and keep her infant daughter with her. She had much to be thankful for.

Lori unlocked the door to the lab, and Beth followed her inside. Within seconds, she had Beth seated with Stevie on her lap.

"All right. Here goes." Lori reached for Stevie's left hand. She swabbed the finger she held and slipped something over the end of it.

Beth watched Stevie's face as she still slept and didn't see Lori puncture the finger. She expected an indignant wail to erupt at any moment, and when it didn't, she turned to see a tiny dot of red stain her baby's finger. Stevie frowned, and she opened her eyes and looked up at her mother as if questioning what had awakened her. Lori scooped the blood into a tiny tube and smiled.

"I'm impressed." Beth spoke softly for fear she would cause a delayed outburst.

Lori looked smug. "Piece of cake. Of course, it helps that she was asleep."

She stuck a colorful bandage on Stevie's finger. "Now I'll go run this through and let you know what type blood our little girl has."

While Lori worked her magic in the lab, Beth fought waves of uncertainty. Sometimes, when problems overwhelmed her, she felt just as she supposed a stepchild would feel. But, of course, she knew God has no stepchildren. And just moments before, she had determined that God was with her. The Gospel of Matthew said He would be—even to the end of the world. Where was her faith?

She told herself everything would be fine. Lori would find out that Stevie was type O, they'd get the hospital to redo the diabetes test, and it would, again, be negative.

"I've got it, Beth, but I don't understand it."

Beth looked up as her friend returned. "What do you mean you don't understand it?"

"Stevie's blood type is AB-positive."

Beth shook her head. "But that's impossible. Lori, I told you, Steven and I both had O-type blood. I'm not a nurse, but even I know we couldn't have a child with AB blood."

What was going on? Beth had expected answers—not more questions.

"Are you sure yours is O?"

Beth slumped against the chair back. This was not the way it was supposed to turn out. She felt as if she had entered the Twilight Zone. She nodded. "Yes, Lori, I know without a doubt that mine is O, and I know Steven's was, too." Her voice wavered. "He always thought it was so neat that we had the same blood type, as if that made us closer or something."

Lori sat in the nearest chair. "Tell me about the day Stevie was born. What went on at the hospital?"

"Night." Beth closed her eyes, remembering. "I went into labor at my parents' house in Blue Springs. They rushed me to the hospital in Kansas City. She was born late that night—well, actually the next morning at twelve twenty-eight."

"What was going on at the hospital?" Lori persisted. "Were you the only one giving birth that night?"

Beth shook her head. "No, there was a woman in the adjoining labor room. I remember hearing her screams, then sudden silence. I guess they gave her something. I really didn't know. Except she died. I heard about it the next day. Her little girl was born within one minute of Stevie. Isn't that strange?"

A look Beth couldn't read crossed Lori's face as she nodded. "Yes, that's very strange." Then she asked, "What else, Beth? Surely there was more happening than just two births."

"Yes, there was. I didn't know about it that night, but a freeway pileup brought so many injured into the hospital that every available doctor and nurse was called in to take care of them. The woman who died giving birth had been in the accident, too. I guess she was in pretty bad shape." Beth gave a laugh without amusement. "I picked a bad time to have a baby."

"You certainly did." Lori looked away.

Beth looked down at Stevie trying to go back to sleep. She tried to smile and found that she couldn't. A tear slid from her eye. Without taking her gaze from the child she loved more than her own life, she spoke. "She isn't mine, is she?"

Lori's voice sounded as if it came from far away. "She's yours, Beth. You've had her all her life."

"Yes, but she isn't the baby I gave birth to." Beth's breath caught in her throat as she choked out, "Lori, where is my baby?"

two

Jonathan McDuff sat in his office at McDuff Family Law and read the letter three times before looking up. He reached for the phone and dialed his home number. On the second ring, his housekeeper picked up. "Hello."

"Mrs. Garrett." Jon's voice carried a hint of steel. "Is Alexis all right?"

"Yes, of course, Mr. Jon. Lexie is fine."

"Is she where you can see her?"

There was a pause on the other end. Mrs. Garrett's voice sounded as if she thought Jon was the one who wasn't all right. "Yes, Lexie is right here playing with her dolls."

"Okay. Thanks." Jon hung up and the tight band that had circled his chest the first time he read the letter eased a bit. He picked it up for a fourth reading.

Some woman in southern Missouri thought Lexie was her child. What kind of fruitcake was she? And what kind of law firm would buy such a story? He inspected the letter to determine if it were official and realized that the embossed letterhead appeared to be as official as his own. He found the phone number for Brewster and Web Law Offices under their name in the letterhead.

Again, Jon reached for his phone and, breathing a prayer to hold his temper in check, he punched in the number. After reaching the secretary, he spent several minutes listening to classical music before a male voice came on the line.

"Yes, this is Gary Web. How can I help you?"

"For starters, you can tell me what kind of scam you and this—" He glanced at the letter on his desk. "—Mrs. Elizabeth

15

Carter are trying to pull."

"Ah, yes." A touch of amusement sounded in Mr. Web's voice. "You must be Jonathan McDuff. Am I correct?"

"Yes, I'm Jonathan McDuff and I don't appreciate this threat against my child."

"Mr. McDuff, I understand that my letter came as quite a shock, but I assure you there is no threat and no scam. According to the blood tests done at the hospital here in Bolivar, Missouri, the baby Mrs. Carter has been raising as her own cannot possibly be hers by birth."

"So what makes you think I have anything to do with her problem?"

"According to the research I personally conducted, your wife gave birth on July 15, one and one-half years ago at the same hospital where Mrs. Carter's baby was delivered, also on July 15, at 12:28 a.m., only one minute from the time your baby was delivered."

He paused and, when Jon didn't respond, continued. "If you will think about it, Mr. McDuff, I believe you will agree that your baby and Mrs. Carter's baby may very well have been switched through an error that night. An error likely caused by the confusion of a freeway pileup that brought more injured in than any hospital should have been expected to handle at one time."

Jon felt the pain that always came as images of that night played in his mind. He and Sharolyn had argued. Sharolyn ran out into the hot summer night threatening to end his baby's life. It was the threat she had used against him repeatedly throughout her pregnancy. Each time, he believed her. She hadn't wanted the baby in the first place and had been furious when he threatened to divorce her and leave her with only enough alimony to squeeze out a living if she got an abortion. He would always wonder if the night she died was the night she had intended to carry through on her threat.

He'd tried to stop her, but before he could reach her, she jumped into her car and sped off into the darkness. He never saw her alive again.

His baby, Alexis Gayle McDuff, had brought meaning back into his life after the sham of his marriage—a marriage that never should have happened. He had entered into his union with Sharolyn at a low point in his Christian faith.

Miraculously, his daughter had lived through the wreck that twisted her mother's car. Without Lexie, Jon didn't know what would have become of him. She was God's gift of love, a gift Jon knew he didn't deserve. But now some woman in a little town in southern Missouri wanted to take her away from him because of some crazy idea that Lexie was switched at birth with her baby? No, he didn't think so.

"Of course, DNA testing will need to be done to prove the parentage of both little girls." Gary Web's voice penetrated his angry thoughts.

Jon frowned. This woman and her lawyer were crazy. Just because his baby was born in the same hospital as hers didn't mean they were switched. No one would be taking Lexie from him. He shook his head and spoke into the phone. "No, I don't think that's necessary."

"Mr. McDuff, we can get court-ordered testing if you refuse to cooperate in a voluntary manner."

Jon sighed. "I'm sure you can. I also know that I can take some time to think about this. To sort out what you've told me. I'll get back with you."

"Fine," Mr. Web said. "If we don't hear from you in two weeks, we will start proceedings to go to court."

Jon didn't give dignity to the threat by answering but hung his phone up and went in search of his father, the senior attorney at McDuff Family Law.

Ray McDuff was discussing a case with Jon's sister, Cecelia Anne, when Jon pushed through the door of his office.

"What's the matter with you, little brother?" Cecelia asked. "You look like a thundercloud about to burst."

"Yeah, maybe I am." Jon thrust the letter at his father but spoke to his sister. "I would say this is private, but since nothing in this family ever is, I might as well save my breath."

"What an astute observation." The pretty brunette smiled. "While Dad reads whatever that is, why don't you tell the best attorney in our firm about it?"

Jon snorted. "That's debatable."

Cecelia laughed. "I'm ready any time you are. Of course you'd lose, you know."

Jon shook his head, refusing to rise to his older sister's jibe. "Sorry, Celia, I think Dad better take this one."

Cecelia's eyes widened. "Oh, really? Then something really is wrong."

"Yeah." Jon turned his attention to his father as the older man lowered the letter.

"Have you ever had any suspicion, any question at all that Lexie might not be your child?"

Jon heard Cecelia's gasp at their father's question. Ignoring her, he shook his head. "None and I still don't. What are the odds that this woman thinks she can get a tidy little sum with this scam?"

"How do you figure that?" Ray asked.

"What are you two talking about?" Cecelia reached for the letter and began reading.

Again Jon ignored her. "Look, Dad. If my marriage taught me nothing else, it taught me that maternal instinct does not always reach beyond the pocketbook. Why else would this woman all of a sudden, after eighteen months, decide that I have her baby? Why not right there at the hospital after the babies were born?"

"Maybe she didn't know until now. Maybe she really wants to see her baby." Cecelia looked up from the letter. "Besides, have you considered that the baby *she* has may very well be your own flesh and blood?"

Jon gave a disgusted sound. He grabbed a picture off his father's desk and thrust it at his sister. "Look at Lexie. What do you see about her that isn't either McDuff or Allen?"

Cecelia frowned as she looked at the portrait of Alexis McDuff at age one. Finally, she shrugged. "I don't know that you can tell for certain. Her coloring is like Sharolyn's, but then that could also be said of a million other people. I always thought she had your smile, but I don't know. I understand that you don't want her to belong to someone else, but how can you be sure?"

"Without the DNA test, you can't," Ray answered for Jon. "I think it would be in the best interest of everyone involved if you submit yourself and Alexis to this testing as soon as possible. Let's get some answers based on fact rather than emotion."

Jon met his father's gaze. "It looks like I'll be in need of an attorney. Are you willing to take the case?"

Ray nodded. "Of course, Son. You know I will."

"Fine." Jon turned toward the door. "Now if you don't mind, I think I'll run home for a few minutes. Lexie was asleep when I left this morning." He paused a second time. "Oh, and I would appreciate your prayers."

෴

Jon pulled into his driveway and sat looking at his house. Built in the Tudor style, it was as different from the house he had shared with Sharolyn as he could find and still stay in a decent neighborhood. After his wife's death, he couldn't live in their house any longer. Everywhere he looked he saw her things, her decorating, her choice of color, everything that belonged to her, and it brought back all the ugliness in their lives. How could he have let his Christian faith slide so much that he would be unequally yoked with a woman who didn't even pretend to be a Christian? He had learned his lesson the hard way. Yet even the sham of their marriage had produced a beautiful little girl.

Jon smiled as he thought of Lexie. He left his car and went inside, where he found his daughter busy in the family room with crayons and coloring book. He peeked around the doorframe and put a finger to his lips so the housekeeper wouldn't warn Lexie of his presence.

"Where's Daddy's girl?" He crouched down to look behind a chair. "Has anyone seen my girl?"

Lexie stiffened at the sound of his voice and turned with eyes wide. As soon as she saw him peering under the chair, calling her name, she put both hands over her mouth and giggled.

Jon glanced across the room at her, then settled his gaze on the housekeeper. "Mrs. Garrett, I seem to have lost Lexie. Do you have any idea where she's gone?"

Mary's short gray curls shook back and forth. "No, Mr. Jon. I don't see her. But she was here just a minute ago."

Lexie bounced and clapped her hands as they both looked under furniture and even in her coloring book, trying to find her. Her soft giggles were a balm to Jon's troubled mind.

When she said, "Dada, I here," he looked directly at her for the first time.

"Here she is, Mrs. Garrett. I found my Lexie girl right in the middle of the room. Now how do you suppose we missed seeing her?"

Mary stood as Jon grabbed his daughter, bringing more giggles to the surface. "I haven't the slightest idea. Now, if you'll excuse me, I'll let you spend a moment together."

Jon scarcely noticed when Mary left the room. His attention was centered on his daughter. His by birth or his by mistake; it didn't matter. Lexie was his alone. No woman had the right to say otherwise.

Then Cecelia's words that morning sounded again in his mind. *Have you considered that the baby she has may very well be your own flesh and blood?*

He hugged Lexie, burying his nose in her clean, baby scent and wondered about the other baby. If she were truly his own child, she would be just as precious to him as Lexie. Something stirred in his heart toward the child he had never seen.

He leaned back and looked at Lexie. "How would you like to go visit the hospital so we can get some questions answered?"

Lexie's large blue eyes brightened. "Go bye-bye."

Jon laughed. "You're always ready to go bye-bye, aren't you? But not just yet. I think the doctor will want us to get an appointment first."

&

A cold March wind blew a gale around Beth's house as she followed Lori outside.

"Make sure Stevie's blanket is over her face." The wind snatched her warning away as soon as it left her mouth, but she saw her friend snuggle the baby closer and knew she had heard.

In the car, Beth turned up the heater while Lori fastened Stevie in her car seat. Lori climbed into the passenger side and shivered. "Brrr. I thought March was supposed to be warmer than this."

Beth smiled. "It *is* warmer than this. The wind just makes it feel cold."

Lori laughed. "I suppose there's some truth in that. I just figure if I feel cold, it's probably because it is cold."

Beth knew Lori talked nonsense to help keep her mind off the one question that had been hounding her. What would happen to them all, now that the DNA test results had come back? Just today, Gary Web had called, then run over to give her a copy of the lab reports. Stevie's biological father was a man named Jonathan McDuff, who lived somewhere in the

Kansas City area, and his baby was indeed her birth daughter.

She had thought that knowing the results would give her a measure of peace. But, she hadn't counted on the trickle of fear that continually chased her thoughts leaving uncertainty behind. How could she build a relationship with a nineteen-month-old child in a couple of hours, a month, or even a week? Eighteen months of growth and development in the McDuff home would have made her baby a McDuff, and a few brief visits would never change that.

"Surely you are not worrying now about your other baby." Lori seemed to read her mind.

Beth pulled to a stop at Highway 13, waiting for the light to change in her favor. She flashed a glance toward her friend. "Why is it that the things you are most anxious to have take the longest to arrive?"

Lori shook her head. "I don't know. We could rationalize that the problem is in our perception. We just think it takes longer because we want them so much. But in this case, you have the results. You know what you suspected is the truth. I would assume then that you can't wait to hold another little darling in your arms. Am I right?"

Beth nodded as she crossed the highway to the restaurant. She pulled into the parking lot and stopped her car before she spoke. "I'm anxious and scared, too, Lori. But the worse of it is that getting into court and reaching an agreement that is acceptable with both of us could take a long time. I don't know how much longer I can wait."

≈

Three days later, Beth still had not heard when her day in court would be. Each day seemed to stretch into forever as she waited for some word from her lawyer. Thursday afternoon was no exception as, one by one, her day-care children left for their own homes until only Debbie and her baby brother had yet to be picked up. The baby was fussy, so Beth settled into the rocking chair to coax him to take some formula and a nap. Just as his eyes drifted shut, the doorbell rang.

Beth breathed a sigh of relief even as Debbie popped up from the floor where she had been playing and said, "Mama."

She loved the little ones, but by the end of the day, Beth was always ready for them to go home. When Debbie's mother didn't come in as she usually did after ringing the doorbell, Beth stood with the baby and went to the door. When she opened it, Debbie pushed past her, then stopped short.

A stranger stood on her doorstep—a tall man in a hat and long coat who somehow made Beth think of the city and theaters and limousines. He looked very out of place on her humble front porch. Her arms instinctively tightened around the baby she held, and she guided Debbie to the side away from him. When she saw it wasn't her mother, Debbie went back to the blocks she and Stevie had been stacking.

"Mrs. Carter?" The man had a nice sounding voice, but at his next words, Beth almost closed the door in his face. "I'm Jonathan McDuff. I wonder if I might have a word with you?"

"Excuse me?" In all her wildest imaginings, Beth could never have guessed that Jonathan McDuff would be standing in front of her just outside her living room. "Do you mean to tell me you are the Jonathan McDuff from Kansas City?"

He inclined his head. "Yes, the very same. Could I step inside? It's been unseasonably cold all week. I'm sure I'm letting your heat escape."

Beth stood her ground, pulling the baby's blanket closer around him. "May I see proof that you are who you say you are?"

Without a word, the man pulled his billfold from his back pocket and flipped it open to reveal his driver's license. Beth looked from the picture to the man and said, "Mr. McDuff,

I was under the impression we would meet in court."

"Ma'am, we aren't enemies. We're both victims of a very strange circumstance, and I'd like to speak with you about it if I may."

Beth looked past him to his late-model SUV parked on the street. The back windows were darkened so that she couldn't see if a baby waited. He must have known what she thought because he glanced over his shoulder and said, "I came alone."

Anger surged through Beth. *How dare he come to see Stevie without bringing the baby!* A cold, stiff wind whistled around the door, blowing the blanket back from the baby she had almost forgotten she still held. Talking through an open doorway would send her heating bill through the roof. She took a step back.

"All right. You may come inside, but I think the first thing you'd better answer is why you didn't bring my baby."

⁊⁊

Jonathan closed the door behind him and took in the sparse furnishings. A sofa and matching chair filled one corner. An entertainment center that probably had come in a box with assembly instructions stood against the opposite wall. The other end of the room, where two little girls about Lexie's age played with some wooden blocks, held built-in cubbies with toys, puzzles, and books sorted in each compartment.

From the investigation his father had done, he knew Mrs. Carter ran a day care in her rented home. She did fairly well, if you could call working twelve hours a day for barely enough to support herself and a baby doing well. He didn't think so, and he doubted Mrs. Carter thought so, either. She could obviously use some extra cash.

"Well?" Beth's voice reminded him she still waited for his explanation. "Where's my daughter?"

Jon frowned. With an emphasis on the first word, he said, "*My* daughter is probably having dinner about now with her grandparents. I did not bring her because I saw no reason to take her out in the cold and upset her routine."

"And what reason did you see to come yourself?" Beth returned to the rocking chair with the baby.

When it seemed she would not extend an invitation, Jon perched on the edge of the sofa. He tried to see Lexie in the woman before him and couldn't. While Lexie had blond hair and blue eyes, Mrs. Carter's hair was as dark as his own. He hadn't noticed her eye color and couldn't see them now.

He shrugged. "I came to take you and your daughter to dinner. I thought it would be beneficial to us both if we met and discussed our mutual problem."

"You mean outside of court?" Suspicion glittered in what he now realized were eyes as blue as Lexie's.

He nodded. Turning on charm had become a lost art to him, but he gave it a try as he smiled. "I have a reservation at a restaurant in Springfield for this evening, and I'd love for you to accompany me. Mrs. Carter, if we are going to work out an arrangement that is satisfactory to us both, we need to maintain a friendly attitude."

Beth rocked the baby for a while before she said, "All right, we'll go with you, but I'll take my own car. I have one more pickup, then we can go."

Jon realized she didn't trust him and admired her for it. He settled back and watched the two little girls play. One stacked some blocks and, while she reached for another, the other child knocked them down. Expecting a howl of displeasure, he was surprised when both little ones laughed and clapped their hands.

The two little girls could have been sisters with their coloring so similar. Both had blond hair and he assumed blue eyes. Actually, if Lexie were here, it would be like having triplets. How could he tell which was his daughter? He looked from one to the other and felt frustration at not knowing. He could pick Lexie out of a hundred little girls, but neither of the two across the room held any special attraction to him. Yet, one was his daughter, born of his own flesh.

While he watched them, the doorbell rang and the door opened. A woman with blond hair rushed in, closing the door behind her, saying, "I will be so glad for spring."

One of the little girls scrambled up and ran to the woman. "Mama."

Jon tuned out the activity as he turned his attention to the remaining child, who now sat watching her friend get ready to leave. So this was his daughter. A feeling of pride gave way to helpless anger that he had been denied this beautiful child. Then he thought of Lexie and his anger faded. He could never wish the last year and a half with her away, even as he could never replace the eighteen months he had lost with his own daughter.

Yet, Lexie was his own daughter, too. He'd like to see anyone try to prove that she wasn't. He watched his birth daughter stand and walk across the floor to Beth's side, and a dart of possessive jealousy struck his heart. She didn't belong with this woman. He wondered if he had enough persuasion to convince her that both babies would be better off with him.

three

"I suppose you expect the baby to ride with you?" Jonathan stood to the side watching Beth balance her daughter in one arm while she locked her front door.

She turned and looked up at him with a frown. What did he think? That she would turn her baby over to him as soon as he showed up at her house? "Of course Stevie is going with me."

"Look, there's really no reason to take two cars. You can ride with me. I'm not Jack the Ripper, after all."

Beth studied his face and eyes. Her mother always said you could tell a lot about a person if you just looked them in the eyes. His eyes were brown. She'd noticed that in the house. Steven had brown eyes and so did Stevie. She'd always thought Stevie had Steven's eyes. Now she knew that wasn't true.

"You have an advantage, Mr. McDuff. By not bringing my baby."

"Lexie is my—" He stopped, his gaze moving to Stevie, and Beth wondered if he felt as confused by the situation as she did. If so, he recovered quickly. "Lexie is better off out of this cold wind just as Stevie will be as soon as we get moving. Please, will you ride with me? I promise I will get you both home safe and sound."

Why was she even going with the man? For a free meal or as a gesture of goodwill? Beth didn't know. But against her better judgment, she heard herself agreeing with him. She even handed Stevie over so Jonathan could buckle her into his car in a car seat that he claimed was hard to operate. She stood watching until he closed the back door. Then he surprised her by opening the passenger door for her.

She sat down and pulled her feet inside. "Thank you."

He nodded and closed the door.

Jonathan pulled onto Highway 13 heading south toward Springfield before the silence grew so loud Beth had to say something. "You said you wanted to get to know Stevie and me. Can you tell me something about yourself? What do you do for a living?"

"I'm an attorney. I work for my father, actually, at McDuff Family Law. We handle estates, divorces, adoptions, family matters for the most part."

"Oh." That one word covered a surge of emotions his disclosure brought. Beth had already guessed from his clothing and late-model automobile that he either had money or was terribly in debt. But she hadn't expected a lawyer. What did that mean for her chances of getting a fair hearing in court? Would he and his father somehow turn the tables on her? At least he would not likely run off with Stevie. He wouldn't have to. No doubt, he knew exactly how to legally take her baby from her.

Jonathan reached for the dash and pushed a couple of buttons. Soft music filled the interior of the vehicle but did little to ease Beth's troubled mind. When he didn't say more, she decided to wait until she could watch his expression before asking any more questions. Thirty minutes later, they reached the city limits of Springfield.

Beth remained silent and so did Jonathan as he turned onto Kearney, then Glenstone. By the time he pulled into the parking lot at the restaurant, Beth wondered how he knew his way around Springfield so well when he lived in Kansas City. Then she looked at her surroundings. As she realized where they had stopped, a flood of memories came back to her.

On their last wedding anniversary—their third—Steven had surprised her by blowing almost a week's grocery budget taking her out to eat at this same restaurant, then to a romantic movie afterward. She would never forget that night and the love she felt for him.

When Jonathan opened the door beside her, Beth realized she had become lost in a time that would never return. She stepped from the SUV and opened the back door while Jonathan closed the front.

"Let me get her out." Jonathan's voice sounded close behind her.

Beth shook her head. "No, she's asleep. If she wakes up to a stranger, it will frighten her."

When he didn't say more or try to stop her, she released the restraint on the car seat. It didn't look that hard to her. She wondered if he said the catch was difficult to operate as an excuse to hold Stevie.

"Come on, sweetheart." Beth pulled her baby from the seat. "It's time to eat supper."

Stevie's head nestled into her shoulder and neck, releasing a current of maternal love that Beth knew would never lessen no matter what the courts decided. She threw the baby blanket over Stevie's head and walked beside Jonathan to the door of the restaurant.

As soon as the waiter left with their order and Stevie was content with a cracker to munch on, Beth looked across the table at Jonathan. "Tell me about my baby."

When his gaze moved to Stevie, she shook her head. "You called her Lexie. Is that her name?"

He turned his full attention on her. "Alexis Gayle McDuff. And let's get something straight. Lexie is very much my daughter."

Just as Stevie is mine. Beth studied the pain-filled eyes before her and wondered what secrets they held. One thing was certain; he loved Lexie just as much as she loved Stevie. He had said they were both victims of an unusual circumstance, and she realized he was right. They were not enemies and should not be fighting. Her heart went out to him.

"I'm sorry. Of course, Lexie is yours after all this time. As Stevie is mine. But on the other hand, don't you agree that Lexie is also my child by birth, just as Stevie is yours?"

Jonathan's expression softened with her apology, and he nodded. "We can't argue with DNA."

"No, we can't." Beth wondered at the edge to his voice. "Do you have a picture of Lexie that I may see?"

"Yes, I do." Jonathan pulled his billfold from his back pocket and opened it. He slipped out a small plastic rectangular insert and handed it to her.

When Beth opened it, a string of accordion-folded pictures fell open. The first was a hospital picture very much like the one Beth had of Stevie as a newborn. Printed across the bottom was *Alexis Gayle McDuff, 6 lbs. 7 oz.*, along with her date of birth, *July 15*. The next picture had been taken at about one month with a new picture each few months after that up to eighteen months. Beth studied each picture carefully, laying them aside when their food arrived.

"Would you mind if I pray?" Jonathan's question surprised but pleased her.

She shook her head. "No, of course not."

Stevie stuck her hand toward Beth. "Pay, Mama."

Beth smiled and took her tiny hand in her fingers. "Yes, sweetie, we are going to pray now."

Beth noticed Jonathan watching them hold hands and expected he would say something, but instead he bowed his head and offered a short prayer of thanksgiving. At least he knew how to pray and was willing to pray in a public place. Although that in itself was not proof of his spiritual condition, Beth wondered if he might be a fellow Christian. He had done nothing to indicate otherwise. He had behaved as a gentleman should since she opened her door and found him standing on her porch. Actually, if the circumstances were different, she thought Jonathan might be someone she would like to know.

"Is Lexie talking yet?" There were so many things she wanted to know about her baby. So much she had missed and could never know.

Jonathan swallowed the food in his mouth and nodded. "About like Stevie. By the way, is that her name? Stevie?"

Stevie looked up at the sound of her name and held her spoon above her head. "Tee-kee."

Jonathan laughed, and Beth sucked in a breath at the dimple that flashed beside his mouth. Stevie's dimple. She closed her eyes as pain ripped through her heart. Now, without a doubt, she knew where Stevie's dimple came from. Beth glanced at her daughter, who thought she had done something funny and was now laughing along with Jonathan. Her dimple flashed in and out as if to say, "Look at me, Mama, I'm not really your baby. I belong to this man."

"Mrs. Carter?" Jonathan's voice sounded concerned. "Is anything wrong?"

Beth forced a smile and blotted her mouth with a napkin to hide its trembling. "No, I'm fine. And to answer your question, yes, that is her name. Stevie Elizabeth Carter. My husband's name was Steven. She's named after her father."

"I see."

Beth's conscience twinged when she realized just how petty that had sounded. Was she trying to get back at him for having a dimple in the exact same place as Stevie's? She picked up the pictures of Lexie and looked through them again. She smiled at one taken outdoors. It appeared the photographer had caught her in a natural pose with her head tilted to one side, her hand digging into her jeans' pocket.

Jonathan leaned closer and spoke. "She has a penny in her pocket."

Beth turned her smile on him. "It's a wonderful picture.

She's a beautiful child."

Jonathan shrugged. "At first I didn't think she looked like you. Now I can see several resemblances. Her eyes for one. They are the same color and shape. And her smile is very like yours."

He couldn't have given her a nicer compliment. Her smile widened. "Thank you. I appreciate you telling me that. Stevie has your eyes and smile, too. I always wondered where that dimple beside her mouth came from."

Jonathan looked at Stevie, and his expression grew soft. "Yes, that dimple is a family trait."

Beth pushed her empty plate away and handed the pictures back to Jonathan as she turned to face him. "There's one thing I don't understand. Why did you come here tonight?"

Jonathan stuffed his pictures back into his billfold. After a moment, his gaze met hers across the table. "I made this trip, Mrs. Carter, to see my daughter and, before the court date is set, I wanted to meet the woman who has cared for her all this time."

"I see."

"Now that I've met you, I'd like to know how you feel about this situation we find ourselves in."

"I really don't understand what you're asking." Beth frowned. "Of course, I was shocked to discover that the child I've always thought was mine is not the baby I gave birth to."

"Exactly." Jonathan nodded. "And what are your feelings about keeping Stevie now that you know she isn't really yours?"

Beth stared at the man sitting across from her. What was he driving at? Surely, he had some motive behind his questions.

She shook her head, trying to clear her thoughts. "But Stevie is really mine. I love her just as if she had been born to me."

"Mrs. Carter, you have no blood tie to Stevie, while I do."

Jonathan still held his billfold in front of him. He glanced down at it, then back up at Beth. "I would be more than willing to recompense any expenses you have incurred in the past year and a half as well as compensate for emotional duress if you will release Stevie into my custody. Furthermore, I would like to legally adopt Lexie."

The blood drained from Beth's face, then rushed back in full force. She thought of the car seat in his car. He expected to take Stevie home with him. Now she understood perfectly. Mr. Rich Lawyer McDuff thought he could buy her baby and steal her birth child all at the same time.

Beth stood, shoving the chair backward. With quick jerks, she grabbed her purse, her baby, their coats, and Stevie's blanket, and headed for the front door.

❧

Jon sat in stunned silence. Whatever was the matter with that woman? Obviously, he had underestimated her. Did she want more than just recompense?

And where did she think she was going? She came with him. He yanked a bill from his billfold and slammed it on the table for a tip. He shoved his chair back as he stuffed his billfold into his pocket. Then he turned and almost ran into a waiter in his hurry to catch up with Beth.

"May I use a telephone?" Jon heard Beth's voice before he saw her. "I need to make a long distance call, but I can pay in advance."

"Oh, no, you don't." Jon stepped in front of her and stood close to her without touching. "You came with me. I promised to get you both home safely, and that's what I intend to do."

"That won't be necessary, Mr. McDuff." Beth stepped back. Her voice sounded colder than the wind felt outside.

"Yes, it's necessary." Jon stood his ground, ignoring the curious stare from the hostess. "What do you intend to do? Call someone in Bolivar to come and get you? You'd have to wait at least an hour for them to drive down here. Stevie doesn't need that."

Jon watched indecision flicker in the depths of Beth's eyes so like Lexie's and knew he had won his case. He stepped back to await the verdict.

"All right. I'll go back with you." Her voice dropped so that he had to lean forward to hear. "And then, I never want to see you again."

≈

The ride back to Bolivar was quiet. Except for Jonathan's choice of music, which Beth found she liked very much, no sound disturbed her troubled thoughts. Why had he tried to take Stevie from her? And Lexie, too. Just as she started to like him, he had to do something so stupid, so demeaning. What could she have possibly done to make him think he could buy her?

Nothing. Because he had come with the intention of talking her into giving up her daughter. He admitted that was why he made the trip. To pay her for allowing him to adopt one baby and take full custody of the other. He wanted to buy Stevie from her. What was she supposed to do? Make a reciprocal payment for his expenses in caring for Lexie? Of course not. He intended to have both babies. Well, he couldn't have Stevie. And she would never let him adopt Lexie.

When Jonathan turned into her driveway and stopped, Beth reached for the door handle. At his voice, she paused.

"Please, tell me something. Why are you so angry?"

"Oh!" Beth made an exasperated sound. "As if you don't know."

She turned in the seat to face him. "Listen, Mr. McDuff, I don't know how things are done in Kansas City, but around here, we don't buy babies."

The shocked look on his face appeared to be real. "I was not offering to buy Stevie. I only offered to reimburse you for the expenses you've incurred for her care."

"As far as I'm concerned, it's the same thing."

He glanced toward her house. "There's a lot you could do with that kind of money."

"Not without Stevie. And that is what you meant, isn't it, Mr. McDuff? You expected me to turn my baby over to you. That's why you brought a car seat. Because you expected to go back to Kansas City with my baby. And you had no intention of ever letting me see Lexie, either." Beth jumped from the car and had the back door open before she shut the front door. She unhooked the belt holding her sleeping baby and lifted her to her shoulder. She grabbed the diaper bag and met Jonathan in front of his car.

With a dignity she didn't feel at the moment, Beth ignored him and marched to her front door. There she fumbled with baby, diaper bag, and key until she felt a hand close over hers.

"I'm sorry I made such a mess of things. Let me at least open the door for you." Jonathan pulled the keys from her hand and unlocked the door.

As she pushed the door open and flipped on her lights, she turned with the pain of disillusionment filling her heart. "What did you expect from me? Did you honestly think that money could possibly take the place of a baby?"

Before he could answer, she took the keys from his hand. "Mr. McDuff, I meant what I said in the restaurant. I don't ever want to see you again."

four

At ten o'clock the next morning, Jon pulled himself from bed. After a sleepless night in a motel room and a couple of tablets to knock the edge from a swelling headache, he headed toward the Brewster and Web Law Offices in downtown Bolivar. Maybe a visit with Mr. Web would straighten out the confusion in his mind about Mrs. Elizabeth Carter.

He parked on the square and made his way to the storefront law office. After giving his name to the receptionist, he eased into one of the metal and vinyl chairs lining the outer wall, then leaned his head against the wall and closed his eyes. Without conscious thought, the vision of Elizabeth Carter came to his mind.

All night he had tried to shake the memory of her eyes so like Lexie's. The hurt in them gripped his heart just as Lexie's baby hurts always brought forth a protective instinct from deep within him. Knowing that he was the cause of Mrs. Carter's pain troubled him. But he'd been so sure she would be willing to discuss the possibility of him taking legal custody of both children if he dangled enough cash in front of her. She hadn't even asked what he considered just recompense. Instead she had grabbed the baby and ran.

"Mr. McDuff?" The receptionist's voice penetrated his troubled thoughts. "Mr. Web will see you now."

Gary Web looked to be about ten years older than Jon. He stuck out his hand with a smile. "Good morning, Mr. McDuff. What can I do for you today?"

Jon shook his hand and sat in the chair he indicated. "I'd like some information. But first I need to tell you that I've been to see Mrs. Carter."

"Oh, really?"

"Yes, last night. I took her and Stevie to dinner in Springfield."

"I see." Mr. Web's eyebrows lifted. "Do you mind telling me what prompted that?"

Jon shrugged. "I wanted to discuss the possibility of adopting Lexie and taking custody of my biological child."

After a chuckle, Mr. Web said, "I'm surprised you're able to tell about it this morning."

Jon didn't see humor in the situation. He frowned. "I offered to pay any expenses she has been out over the past year and a half."

Mr. Web laughed before apologizing. "I'm sorry. You see, I attend the same church Beth does, so I know her fairly well. My guess is that she is pretty steamed at you about now. Am I right?"

Jon nodded.

"Did you honestly expect her to hand over the baby she's raised from infancy for a few dollars? Or any amount, for that matter. And by the way, I'm sure you know that buying babies is illegal not to mention immoral. But let me ask you this. I understand your wife is no longer living. If she were, would she have given up her baby? Would your mother have?"

"My wife? Yes. My mother? No." Jon looked across the desk at Mr. Web. "Not all women have a strong maternal instinct. To such women, money is more important than a child that is not theirs in the first place. And get this straight. I was not offering to buy the baby. I know Mrs. Carter has limited income and, since Stevie is not actually her child, I merely suggested she allow me to relieve her of the burden of the child's care and custody. That alone should relieve her financial difficulties. Paying back expenses would only be fair."

"I see. And now you know that Beth is like your mother—

not your late wife." Mr. Web leaned back in his chair. "Let me tell you something about Beth. When she first came to me, I encouraged her to bring suit against the hospital. She refused, saying she understood how the error was made. She said the hospital was not at fault. Instead, circumstances, the confusion of the freeway pileup, and probably one nurse's error caused the switch. No amount of money would entice her to cause pain to another person. I don't know what your intentions are regarding the hospital, but Mrs. Carter will not sue. Her concern is for the babies. Just as I believe yours is."

Jon sat for several minutes trying to take in this new picture of motherhood, which he realized was nothing like Sharolyn had been from the time she discovered she was pregnant. His father's investigation had uncovered Beth's financial situation but had not touched on her heart and soul. Now he realized she was more than a struggling, single mother who barely met the bills each month. She was a mother in the true sense of the word. Like his own mother.

Shame washed through him, and he stood to shake hands with the lawyer. "Thank you for your time and your advice. I can see now that what I did was wrong and not well thought out. Although my intentions were not to buy a child but to simply bring my child home where she belongs, I can see where Mrs. Carter may have gotten the wrong idea. I suppose I would be just as angry if the tables were turned. I love Lexie as if she had been born to me. Mrs. Carter obviously feels the same way toward Stevie."

Mr. Web nodded. "Yes, she does."

≈

Jon stepped out on the sidewalk just as the sun peeked from behind a blanket of clouds. He had been so convinced that Mrs. Carter needed and wanted money. And he had assumed she would be like his wife. Maybe not eager to be rid of the baby, but at least willing to discuss the possibility. He walked to his car and unlocked the door. As he got in and inserted his key, he realized that Sharolyn still held power over him. Somehow, she had convinced him that all women were like her. But they weren't. How could he have forgotten his mother or his sister?

He drove slowly through the streets of the small town, going ever farther from the busy hub of the square. When he stumbled upon a park in the north part of town, he pulled into the deserted parking area and stopped. There he could see water from a small lake glistening in the sunshine. A swan and several white geese swam across the surface. Reminded of a similar lake in the park near his home, he climbed from his car. The tranquil movement of water had a calming effect on him when life's troubles pressed too close.

Jon sat on the bank and stared at the rippling water as a warm breeze touched its surface. Strange how the weather could change so quickly from freezing cold the night before to sunshine and warm breezes the next day. *Just like a woman*, he thought. He wondered about Mrs. Carter. Was she as changeable as Sharolyn had been? Not that Sharolyn had ever changed her mind about wanting their baby. She hadn't. But she had been a master at freezing him out one minute, then snuggling against him the next. Anything to get her way.

For several minutes, Jon watched the water lap gently against the bank of the lake. He breathed a prayer for direction. What should he do about the two little girls? Sitting back while the courts decided where the girls belonged would not be sufficient. Surely, there was something he could do to assure that both Lexie and Stevie would be a part of his life. From what he'd learned about Mrs. Carter, she wouldn't be content with visits, either. Actually, he was surprised she hadn't tried to get custody of both babies. If Gary Web knew her as well as he thought he did, the babies were of paramount importance to her. So much so that she might—

Jon's mind whirled as a new possibility occurred to him. It just might work. If only he could figure out the details, then convince Mrs. Carter that it was the best way. If she agreed to his plan, they would both win.

Jon stayed by the lake praying for wisdom as he went over details in his mind and trying to foresee any possible complications. Finally, a rumble in his stomach reminded him that it was well past the noon hour. He glanced at his watch. Four more hours until six o'clock—the time when he assumed Mrs. Carter closed her day care. It had been about that time last night when the last two children had been picked up. He wanted her full attention when he presented his proposal so he'd wait until straight up six before dropping in on her. In the meantime, he'd grab a bite to eat, then try to get some rest.

❧

Beth kept the swings going for her two- and three-year-olds while she watched the rest of the children, especially Stevie. With the children's excited calls and laughter as they tried to release an entire winter's pent-up energy in the space of one warm morning, Beth was afraid she might not hear an intruder. She didn't really believe that Mr. McDuff would try to kidnap Stevie. She gave him more credit than that. But she knew of the dogged determination Stevie displayed when she wanted something. Mr. McDuff hadn't finished what he came to Bolivar to do. Beth knew it as well as she knew that Stevie had inherited her stubborn streak from someone besides her or Steven.

Beth let the swings slow to a stop and pulled the sleeping baby from his infant swing. She adjusted the blanket around him and started toward the back door. "Let's everyone line up. It's time to go inside."

"I'm stayin' outside." Three-year-old Jack turned to go the opposite direction.

Beth sighed. Every day Jack pushed the limits. According

to the state guidelines, three-year-olds could play unattended outdoors, but she doubted they had Jack in mind when they made that rule.

"That's fine, Jack. You may stay outside and play alone while the rest of us go inside to paint a picture."

As she expected, the other children quickly got into line, chattering and asking questions about the painting they would be doing. They followed her to the door, while Jack took a few minutes to make his decision before trailing after them.

Painting supplies waited in the kitchen where Beth had left them the night before. Allowing the children to paint in the kitchen served two purposes. Cleanup was easier, and she could fix lunch while they were occupied in the same room with her.

"Sit around the tables while I put the baby in his bed." Beth watched for just a moment while Jack jostled another child to get the seat he wanted. When no fight broke out, she stepped through the dining room and into the living room, where the baby's playpen stood.

She carefully lowered the sleeping baby, then stood, and looked out the window to the street beyond. No silver SUV was in sight in either direction. Beth breathed a sigh of relief and went back into the kitchen.

Beth made sure all the children had a plastic apron over their clothing, then she handed out the paper and small bowls of her own homemade paint made of food coloring, soap, and corn starch mixed with water. While the children smeared red, blue, and yellow streaks across their paper, Beth started water boiling for noodles.

By the time lunch was ready, her small artists had tired of painting and were ready to help clean up so they could eat. Beth hung the paintings by clothespins to a small umbrella line she kept in the corner for that purpose. Four-year-old

Amanda placed the freshly washed brushes in a cup and put it on a shelf in the corner.

After lunch, while the children slept, Beth played on the floor with the now wide-awake four-month-old and listened for the sound of a motor outside. After several minutes of starting every time a vehicle passed, she moved to the rocker in front of the window so she could see both the street and her driveway. She looked out at the empty street and almost wished Mr. McDuff would show up. At least then she could stop worrying that he might.

The children woke from their naps and he hadn't come. When Jack left at three o'clock, Beth looked out the door. Still no sign of a silver SUV. By the time Debbie and her baby brother left at six o'clock, Beth began to wonder if Jonathan McDuff had gone back to Kansas City. Maybe he had taken her seriously when she'd told him she didn't want to ever see him again. She hoped so but somehow doubted it.

Beth picked up her little daughter and gave her a hug. "How would you like to go see Aunt Lori tonight?"

Stevie nodded her head with a big grin. She jabbered something in her own baby language that Beth didn't catch.

All she could see was her baby's lone dimple. The dimple she had thought was so cute before now served as a stark reminder that their lives were no longer their own. As much as she longed for the baby she had given birth to, she dreaded the day she would have to hand Stevie to Jonathan McDuff and watch him walk away with her—even if only for a few minutes.

The thought spurred her into action as she grabbed the diaper bag on her way out the door. She knew she should have called Lori first, but she hadn't planned to run away until the last minute. She pulled to a stop in front of Lori's ranch-style house and looked at the closed garage door. Not knowing whether the door shielded a car or an empty garage,

Beth turned to Stevie.

"Mama's going to see if Aunt Lori's home. Okay? I'll be right back."

Stevie nodded, her large brown eyes showing trust that Beth knew she didn't deserve. Then Stevie mimicked, "Back." And her baby smile warmed Beth's heart.

Keeping the car and her baby within sight, Beth pounded on Lori's door. If she wasn't home or didn't have time for them tonight, Beth didn't know what she would do. One thing was for certain, she didn't plan to return home and confront Mr. McDuff.

After what seemed longer than it probably was, Lori opened the door with a smile.

"Hi, what are you doing here? Is Stevie in the car?"

"Yes, is it all right if we come in? I thought you might like to take in a movie or something tonight."

Lori shrugged as her eyes narrowed. "Sure, it sounds like fun. What's going on?"

"Why does something have to be going on? Can't I goof off once in a while?"

Lori laughed. "Goof off, yes. But you act like you're scared of something. You know, like a monster is after you."

Beth glanced at her car again. "Let me get Stevie, then I'll tell you what's been going on."

❧

One pizza and two movies later, Beth packed a very sleepy Stevie into her car. Lori trailed behind carrying the diaper bag. She remained silent until Beth closed the back door and turned to take the bag.

When Lori handed it to her, she said, "It's going to be all right, Beth."

Beth blinked against the stinging in her eyes. She nodded. "I know. I keep telling myself that. Then I look at Stevie and I realize that I'm going to lose her. I'll have to share her with her real family, Lori. What's she going to think when she's old enough to understand? Maybe she'll want to live with them. Maybe she won't want anything to do with me after she's met them and she knows they are hers in a way I'll never be."

Lori touched Beth's shoulder in a gesture of comfort. "You are the only mother Stevie has ever had. I know this is a mixed-up mess, but God knows what He's doing, Beth. Don't ever think He doesn't care about you. You will always be Stevie's mother—in her heart and yours, too. And now you have another baby."

"Mr. McDuff may remarry."

"So what?" Lori gave Beth a quick hug. "You probably will, too. And that will just give the girls two more parents to love."

"One more. I'll never find anyone who can make me forget Steven." Beth opened the car door and slipped inside. She smiled up at Lori. "But I'll try to hold to your optimism when Mr. McDuff confronts me as I know he will. I'm surprised he didn't come today."

"Maybe he's given up and gone home."

Beth's laugh was not as cheerful sounding as she would have liked. "You are the optimist, Lori. Mr. McDuff is probably just as determined to have his way as Stevie always is. You know how she can be. He wants her, and I'll bet the only reason he didn't show up today is because he's been trying to figure out the best way to get her away from me."

With Lori's reassurances ringing in her ears, Beth drove the short distance to her own house. Maybe she should have stayed home. A confrontation might have been better than looking over her shoulder all the time, hoping there was no one there.

She glanced at her watch as she drove under a streetlight and saw that it was just after ten o'clock. At least she wouldn't have to worry about him stopping by this late at night. She breathed easier until she turned on her street and saw the dark shape of a vehicle parked near her house. Her headlights picked up the silver color as she reached her driveway.

Although she was tempted to keep driving, Beth steeled herself for the inevitable. She'd have to confront Mr. McDuff sometime. It might as well be tonight. She turned into her driveway and watched her headlights sweep the front of the house. A man sat on her porch swing waiting. He lifted his head to watch her come to a stop at the end of the driveway.

five

Beth glanced back at Stevie and saw that she was asleep. It wouldn't hurt to leave her in the car while she got rid of Mr. McDuff. She climbed from her car and closed the door with a soft click. She could feel his gaze on her as she stepped across the yard to the porch.

"I told you last night—"

"I know what you said last night, Mrs. Carter. However, I would like to talk to you about something important."

He stood, forcing her to step up on the porch so she didn't feel intimidated by his superior height. "Mr. McDuff, Stevie is my daughter and I will not give her to you."

The streetlight cast just enough light on her porch that she could make out the features on his face. She saw a faint smile touch his lips before he spoke.

"As much as I'd like for that to happen, I realize now that it isn't going to. Is Stevie in the car?"

"Yes, she's asleep."

"Shouldn't she be in bed?"

Beth bristled at what she considered criticism from a man who had no right to criticize anything she did. "Of course, she should be in bed. And she will be just as soon as you leave so I can get her there."

A ragged sigh tore from Jonathan's throat. He shook his head. "I suppose I deserve that. Would it help if I told you again that I'm sorry? I misjudged you, and you can't imagine how awful I feel about my actions. Please, may I come inside where we can talk? I promise I won't stay long."

Beth realized he had no intention of leaving until he had his say. She could force him to talk on the porch, but she didn't want to leave Stevie in the car that long. Besides, the porch was so dark, she couldn't read the expression in his eyes.

"All right. I'll get Stevie." She sorted through the ring of keys she still held in her hand. "Here is the key to the front door. Would you mind unlocking it for me?"

Beth left Jonathan in the living room while she put Stevie to bed. When she came back, he stood from the couch. She sat in a swivel rocker across the room from him, and he sat back down. So chivalry was not dead. Beth tried to think of any other man who stood when she entered a room and drew a blank. Steven had never been one to open doors and such for her, but she had always attributed that to his illness. She knew most of the time he didn't feel well, and she had naturally stepped into the role of caregiver. She had to admit it was refreshing to be treated with such respect. Mr. McDuff made her feel more feminine than she had in a long time.

"Would you like anything, Mr. McDuff? I have coffee or hot chocolate."

"If it's no trouble, hot chocolate sounds pretty good."

"No trouble at all." As Beth expected, when she stood, so did Jonathan. What she didn't expect was for him to follow her to the kitchen.

He leaned against the doorframe and watched her fix two cups of hot chocolate. When she set the steaming mugs on the table, he pulled a chair out for her, then sat across from her. He was the first to speak.

"I've done a lot of thinking since last night. We aren't enemies—or shouldn't be." He smiled, letting that dimple so like Stevie's deepen. "Would you be interested, Mrs. Carter, in having both babies in your care?"

Beth almost choked on her drink. Whatever was this man talking about? Last night he wanted to take Stevie from her. Was he now offering to give Lexie to her? She knew her face mirrored her shock when he held up a hand and shook his head.

"Don't worry, I'm not about to give my daughter away. I'm offering you a job caring for both our girls in my house. I'll pay you a salary plus give you and Stevie room and board."

Beth's eyes narrowed and she shook her head. "You would create a job for me just so you can have Stevie in your home?"

Jonathan's eyebrows lifted and his gaze grew intense. "Yes, I would if I had to. But the job is very real. At the moment, my housekeeper watches Lexie while I work. She keeps the house clean, cooks the meals, and baby-sits my daughter. Don't you think she has more than enough to do?"

Beth laughed as much from nerves as from the humor in his question. "Of course she does, and I'm sure any housewife would tell you the same."

Jonathan looked at her for just a moment before he laughed with her. Beth liked the sound of his laughter. Even his dimple didn't bother her so much this time, and that surprised her.

"But Mrs. Garrett is an employee and as such she shouldn't be expected to work twenty-four hours a day."

"I'm sure that's true." Beth took another sip of her hot chocolate as she tried to absorb what had just been thrown at her. Did he really want her to live in his house and care for both girls as her own? The entire concept was too much like a dream come true to be real. Surely there was a catch somewhere. Of course, the biggest obstacle sat across the table from her. Mr. McDuff would be there every day interfering with Stevie. As her employer, he would have the right to insist that she do things his way, raise her daughter—his daughter—the way he wanted. Could she give up her freedom for Lexie? For the daughter she had yet to see?

"You will have your own room upstairs next to the nursery. If you have no objections, we can let the girls room together. And, if it helps, I'll be downstairs. There's a bedroom just off my den. Mrs. Garrett has always slept upstairs near the girls."

Beth had a feeling that sleeping arrangements in the McDuff house would be quickly shuffled if she accepted his offer. She stirred her hot chocolate, keeping her gaze away from him. Even with another woman there all the time, how could she live in the same house with a man who posed so great a threat to Stevie? Yet how could she turn away from the only chance she would likely ever get to raise both of her daughters—to be with them every day and to watch them grow?

"I will match the income you get here, in your day care."

Beth lifted her gaze to see Jonathan glance around her kitchen. Apparently not missing anything, he looked from the dishes still draining by the sink to the small tables and benches in the corner. He looked up at Stevie's painting hanging by the clothespin above the tables. His gaze locked on it, and he stood to take a better look. Two steps took him to the painting. He lifted the curled edge and a faint smile touched his lips.

"Stevie did this, didn't she?"

Beth nodded. "The other kids took theirs home. I usually put her artwork on the refrigerator for a few days before I put it away."

When he turned and looked at her, Beth saw the haunted look in his eyes and knew what he would ask.

"Would you miss just this one if I took it? You must have dozens like it."

And what can you give me of Lexie's? Beth thought the words but couldn't say them. As much as she wanted to be spiteful and mean to him, she couldn't. Jonathan McDuff was Stevie's birth father. Without him, she would have never known and loved Stevie. And now he was offering her the chance to establish a relationship with Lexie, as well. As the girls' primary caregiver, she would be able to fulfill the role of mother with both babies.

She met Jonathan's gaze and nodded. "Yes, you may take it with you. You are right. I do have several more."

His quick smile brought warmth to her heart. She found herself smiling back even as she wondered if Jonathan McDuff always got what he wanted.

He returned to the table and, still standing, finished his now cooled drink. "I should be going. I didn't expect an answer to my offer tonight. Why don't you think about it this next week? I'm leaving in the morning for the city, but I'll be back next Saturday morning to take you and Stevie home with me for the weekend. That is, if you will go?"

Beth stared at him, then slowly shook her head. "Do you ever slow down? I feel like I'm on a merry-go-round that won't stop spinning. It's been that way ever since I opened the door last night and found you on the other side."

"Does that mean I can expect you to be ready when I get here Saturday?" Jonathan's grin had Beth laughing when she should have felt anger instead.

"Are you giving me a tour of the house before I decide to move?"

Jonathan nodded. "Yes, ma'am. I expect you to enjoy the weekend. Did I mention that if you should decide to accept the job, your only required chores will be the care of the babies?" He indicated the dishes in the drainer. "No cleaning, cooking, or dishes to do."

Beth sobered. "That sounds wonderful, but I'm sure you know the only reason I will accept. I want Lexie in my arms just as much as you want Stevie in your possession."

The expression on Jonathan's face hardened, and his voice sounded almost angry as he asked, "Would it be too much trouble for me to tell Stevie good-bye on my way out the door?"

"She's asleep." Beth searched his face, startled by the change in his attitude.

"I won't wake her. I just want to see her once more before I leave."

Beth shrugged. "All right. I suppose it won't hurt anything."

Without another word, Jonathan turned toward Stevie's bedroom, and Beth followed. She stood in the doorway watching as he lowered the side of Stevie's baby bed without making a sound. He then bent over and placed a soft kiss on her forehead.

When he remained motionless, looking down at the sleeping baby in the soft glow of the nightlight, Beth wondered if he found it hard to say good-bye to the daughter he had just found. Although he hadn't seemed to pay much attention to Stevie, Beth had caught him watching her the few times they were together. Now he seemed reluctant to leave, and Beth wondered if Jonathan McDuff hurt inside just as much as she did.

Before he left, Beth stopped Jonathan in the living room. "Will you have Lexie tested for diabetes?"

He frowned. "Why?"

"Her father was diabetic as a child. He died from complications of the disease. It can be hereditary. The test is a simple blood test."

Jonathan was silent so long, Beth thought he would brush her concerns aside. When he nodded, she released the breath she had been holding. "All right, I will. As soon as possible."

Beth closed the door behind Jonathan and headed for the telephone. She realized how late it was as she punched in her friend's phone number and hoped that Lori hadn't gone to bed yet. A nervous excitement stirred within Beth as she waited for Lori to answer.

So much had happened in her life recently. But nothing compared with the thought of seeing and holding her own baby for the first time.

When Lori's voice came on the line, Beth told her all about

Jonathan's visit and his invitation for the weekend.

"Are you going?"

Beth laughed. "What do you think? Do you think I would miss the chance to see Lexie?"

Lori laughed. "No, I don't." Her voice grew soft then. "I'll miss you, Beth. You and Stevie both."

"We'll just be gone until Sunday evening."

"No, I mean after that. Within the month, you will be living in Kansas City. But I want you to know, I'd do the same thing if I were in your place."

"Lori, I haven't made up my mind about that."

"Haven't you really, Beth?"

Beth remained quiet as she thought of what it would mean to take Jonathan up on his offer. She would be making the same income but without the expense of running a day care. And surely taking care of two little girls would be easier than putting up with Jack Helm—not to mention caring for up to ten children every day. But none of that mattered, really. What did matter was that she would be with both her children.

She laughed aloud. "Do you know what's funny, Lori?"

"No, what's that?"

"Jonathan McDuff has offered me a cushy job with good pay and what he doesn't know is that I'd be willing to pay him for the privilege of having both babies in my care twenty-four hours a day, seven days a week."

six

Beth woke the next Saturday with nervous fluttering in her stomach. She glanced at the bedside clock and groaned. Mr. McDuff would arrive in less than two hours. How could she have slept so late? She pushed the tangled covers aside and climbed from bed. No doubt the restless night she'd just spent trying to visualize her baby might have had something to do with it. Would Lexie look like her or Steven? From the pictures she'd seen, she had his blond hair. But her eyes were blue—like Beth's.

Beth grabbed a pair of black slacks and a blue checked blouse from the closet, some underwear from the drawer, then headed for the shower. She had just enough time to shower and dress before Stevie demanded her attention.

Two hours later, Beth had Stevie fed and dressed in jeans and long-sleeved T-shirt. Her baby-fine hair was just long enough to put up in matching pigtails secured with blue ribbons to match her shirt.

Although she'd been looking for the silver SUV each time she went near a window, Beth jumped when her doorbell rang. Somehow, she had missed the sound of either the motor or a car door closing.

When she opened the door, Jonathan smiled. "Are you ready to go?"

"Go bye-bye." Stevie toddled toward him with her arms up.

Jonathan laughed and crouched down to the baby's level. With a quick glance toward Beth, he scooped Stevie up and held her close before standing again with the baby in his arms.

"You sound just like Lexie. She loves to go bye-bye, too."

Stevie turned toward Beth, one arm reaching, her fingers motioning for her to come. "Bye-bye, Mama."

Beth's heart had almost stopped when Stevie went to Jonathan so easily. Now she felt the blood rush back into her face, and she was able to move. Everything they needed for the weekend was packed and sitting by the door. She picked up the diaper bag and her purse and reached for the overnight bags when Jonathan stopped her.

"Here, let me get those."

"But, Stevie. . ."

The smile he flashed at her weakened her resolve. "I can carry Stevie and a couple of bags. Don't worry, Mrs. Carter, I'm used to it. I have a good hold on our little sweetheart. I won't drop her."

Our little sweetheart? Beth wasn't sure she liked being linked together with Mr. McDuff. Even the common bond they had in their two children hadn't warned her that the two of them would be brought close. But if she moved into the same house with him, wouldn't they at the very least occasionally bump into each other?

Beth followed Jonathan and Stevie to the car, and for the first time since she'd met him, she looked at him as a man. She noticed he wore designer jeans and a lightweight jacket over his polo shirt. The description "tall, dark, and handsome" fit him perfectly. Probably in his early thirties, with thick, dark brown hair and a lean body build, Jonathan McDuff would turn the heads of most women.

He kept Stevie sitting in the crook of his arm and set the bags beside his automobile while he opened the door. He lowered Stevie into the car seat and gave her a quick kiss on the top of her head, earning a dimpled grin in the process.

Beth noticed the pleased look on his face when he reached for the bags to put them in the back. She stuck the diaper bag on the floor in front of Stevie, where it would be handy before settling in the front passenger seat.

As Jonathan scooted behind the wheel, he smiled at her. "I thought you might like to know that Lexie tested negative for diabetes."

"Oh, yes!" Beth closed her eyes and breathed a silent prayer of thanksgiving.

"If you don't mind, I'd like to pray before we go," Jon said. "Since my wife's death, I've made a habit of praying before I start anywhere."

Beth looked at him in surprise and nodded. "I think that's a wonderful idea. Actually, everyone should do the same."

"Thanks for understanding." Jonathan bowed his head and Beth followed suit.

As they got on the way, Stevie played with her sippy cup and a few toys that Beth provided. Beth leaned her head against the seat back and tried to relax. Jonathan's classical music soothed her jangled nerves, and she wondered how he managed to stay awake and drive. The three-hour drive to the city seemed to take forever, yet as traffic increased and Beth saw the Belton city limits sign, she wished for more time.

"Do we need to stop for anything?" Jonathan's voice startled her and she straightened.

"Actually, a diaper check might be in order." Beth glanced back at Stevie, who appeared to be wide awake and interested in the new sights outside her window.

Jonathan nodded. "Yes, I can imagine. Can you change her in here or do I need to find something more convenient? That station ahead looks like a good place to stop."

"Any place is fine. I can change her on my lap if I need to."

Jonathan shot a doubtful look Beth's way before he turned off the highway and stopped to the side of the service station parking lot. "Will this be all right?"

Beth nodded. "Yes, it's fine. Thank you."

"Good. I'll see what I can find inside. What would you like to drink?"

Beth hesitated, not willing to take anything from Jonathan. Then she mentally shrugged. If she was going to work for him, what would it hurt to accept a soft drink from him? "Sprite would be fine."

Within minutes, they were back on the road going ever deeper into the city. Beth recognized a few landmarks from her childhood, but for the most part she felt as if she were in a completely different world. She had grown up in Blue Springs, a community separated from the municipality that made up greater Kansas City. She realized from her stay with her parents a year and a half earlier that the city was rapidly surrounding Blue Springs as well, and she regretted the loss of her hometown's small-town feel.

She thought of Bolivar and knew she would miss the quiet and peaceful life she had lived there. She watched the vehicles zoom past in the opposite lanes. The ones headed in the same direction that they traveled reminded her of horses in a race. A car drove alongside them taking the lead one minute and falling back the next. Could she get used to the rush of the city? Did she want to? She thought of the baby waiting for her in Jonathan's house and felt the tension ease. Yes, she could adjust to anything if only she could hold her baby in her arms and watch her grow to womanhood.

By the time Jonathan turned off the four-lane highway and drove into the slower pace of a residential area, Beth could scarcely sit still. When they entered a well-kept neighborhood with large beautiful houses centered in spacious green lawns, Beth knew they were nearing the McDuff house. He pulled into a drive and stopped behind a forest green van.

"Looks like we have a welcoming committee." Jonathan shook his head, looking none too pleased. "The van belongs to my sister, Cecelia. As oldest in the family, she thinks she has to take care of me."

As an only child, Beth could not appreciate Jonathan's problem with his sister. She also had not considered the fact that there would be extended family to deal with so quickly. The flutters returned to her stomach as she followed Jonathan's lead and climbed from the vehicle.

Stevie was ready to leave the confines of her car seat, but Beth didn't feel ready to face what lay behind the walls of Jonathan's gray stone, two-story house. She pulled Stevie from the backseat and sat on the front seat with the door open and Stevie on her lap.

"Let's get your hair straightened out. We don't want to go meet a bunch of new people with messy hair, do we?"

Stevie arched her back, trying to get down. Beth hauled her back on her lap and, with a tight hold to keep her there, she smoothed and tightened the pigtails that had looked much better that morning. Thankfully, Stevie's protests were token at best. Beth knew she could throw a much better tantrum.

"She looks fine." Jonathan stood to the side with the bags in his hand. His other hand rested on the open door.

When Beth looked up at him and noticed the faint smile that softened his face, she wondered if he understood just how she felt. If anyone could, surely it would be him.

She sighed. "I suppose she'll have to do."

"Don't worry. It's just my sister and Mrs. Garrett. We know Lexie will love you, don't we?"

Beth looked quickly at him but could read nothing in his expression that would explain that remark. "Why did you say that?"

Pain flickered in the depths of his dark eyes, and he shrugged. "You're her mother, aren't you? It won't take long for Lexie to realize that."

"Just as you are Stevie's father. You think that's why she

went to you so quickly this morning?"

Again he shrugged. "Maybe."

Beth stood and walked beside Jonathan to the house. She carried Stevie, and childish as it was, she kept her to the side away from Jonathan.

A woman who Beth judged to be in her late fifties opened the door for them before they were halfway across the front porch.

Jonathan grinned. "You must have been watching out the window."

The woman smoothed the apron over her ample middle and laughed. "Just for the last hour. Cecelia's here, too. We've been anxious to meet our new addition to the family."

"Mrs. Garrett, this is Mrs. Carter." Jonathan introduced them.

"Beth, please." Beth expected to shake hands and was surprised to receive a quick hug instead.

"Then, I'm Mary. You can't imagine how excited we all are." Mary's smile covered her entire face. "I'm so glad you are here, Beth. And I'm anxious to meet this baby."

Stevie ducked her head into Beth's shoulder at the sudden attention, and the adults laughed.

Mary patted her on the back. "Don't you worry. We'll be the best of friends. Just like your sister and I are."

Sister? Beth felt as if a glass of cold water had been thrown into her face. But Stevie and Lexie were sisters of a sort, weren't they? She had been so busy thinking of her relationship with both babies, she hadn't thought of how the girls would feel. What if they hated each other? Jealousy between the girls, especially as they grew older, could be a very real problem.

"I'll bet you are eager to meet your daughter." Mary's voice penetrated Beth's concerns. "She's in the kitchen with her aunt. I'll let you go ahead while I finish with lunch."

Beth moved down the hall and through a formal dining

room to the kitchen door with the others. At the door, Jonathan stepped back. "I'll take your bags upstairs to your room. You go ahead and get acquainted with Lexie."

Beth nodded and watched him walk away. She didn't know whether she felt abandoned or thankful for his consideration in letting her meet her daughter for the first time without having to compete with him for her attention. As she stepped into the kitchen, she decided to be thankful.

Beth sought her daughter. She scarcely noticed when Mary went into the immaculate kitchen, which was separated from the dining area by a long, curved, breakfast bar. A woman, probably in her mid thirties, sat at the table facing a high-chair. Lexie, blond hair and blue eyes, stared at the newcomers. Beth's breath caught in her throat. This was Steven's child. Large blue eyes, so like Beth's own, looked with a solemn appraisal at her. But the features were Steven's, altered and softened in her baby face. Beth felt sure she would have known her anywhere.

"You must be Mrs. Carter." The woman spoke as she stood to remove the tray from the highchair. "I'm Jon's sister, Cecelia."

"Hello. I'm pleased to meet you." Beth tried to smile at the woman but couldn't take her eyes from her daughter.

"And that must be Stevie." Cecelia lifted Lexie from the highchair and crossed the room where Beth stood with a tight grip on Stevie. "I couldn't wait to meet my new niece, so here I am. I hope you don't mind. We've all been on pins and needles ever since Jon found out about her. Here, why don't we see if Lexie will go to you?"

Beth seldom had trouble coaxing a child from their mother, but this was different. If Lexie turned away from her or cried, it would break her heart. She forced a trembling smile and held out her hand.

"Hi, Lexie." More than anything, she wanted to touch her

baby. To count her fingers and toes. To turn back the clock and do all those things that new mothers have done for generations when they were first introduced to their offspring. All the things that had been denied her and Lexie.

Stevie patted Beth's face and pointed to Lexie. "Mama, baby."

"Yes, I see, sweetheart. Another baby just your age. This is Lexie." Beth reached a tentative hand toward Lexie and stroked her arm. The hint of a smile brightened Lexie's serious face. Beth took that as encouragement and her smile grew stronger.

She wiggled her fingers for Lexie to come. "May I hold you, Lexie? Will you come and see me?"

When Lexie's little arms reached toward her, Beth could scarcely contain the joy that surged through her heart. She reached for her as Cecelia sat her on her arm. Beth brought both her daughters close for a heartfelt embrace. She closed her eyes, reveling in the feel of their tiny bodies in her arms. Never before had she experienced such a wondrous thing.

"May I hold Stevie?" Cecelia's voice brought her back to the realization that she was not the only one who had some catching up to do.

"Oh, I'm sorry. Of course you may." Beth nodded toward Cecelia. "Stevie, this is your aunt."

Cecelia reached for Stevie, and after a short hesitation, Stevie leaned into her embrace. Cecelia gave her a quick kiss, then said, "Why don't we sit down here at the table and get better acquainted?"

While Cecelia talked to Stevie, telling her all about the rest of the family, Beth made friends with Lexie. As she talked to the baby and let her play with her watch, Beth felt as if she were on a roller coaster ride of emotions. Overwhelming love for the baby in her arms surprised her—even as fear that her love would be rejected tried to gain a foothold. . .accompanied by a rush of anger that this beautiful child had been taken from her.

Beth held Lexie's tiny hand in her fingers and ran her thumb over each perfectly formed nail. She could hear Stevie's chatter as she talked to her aunt and smiled. Lexie had not uttered one word in all the time she held her. Whether she was just shy or she couldn't talk as well as Stevie, Beth didn't know. What she did know was that she loved Lexie even more than she had expected to.

"How are we getting along?" Jonathan came through the open doorway.

Beth looked up with a smile and met his gaze. "Even better than I expected."

Something flickered in his eyes as he looked from her to Lexie and back. A faint smile touched his lips as he squatted in front of her. "Glad to hear it."

"Dada." Lexie launched herself toward her father, leaving Beth's arms empty.

২৯

After lunch, Cecelia excused herself and left, saying she had an appointment that afternoon. Jonathan walked out with her as Mary brought two damp washcloths to the table and handed one to Beth. With a smile, she asked, "Which of these dirty faces would you like to wash?"

Beth looked from one baby to the other. Mashed potatoes radiated from the mouths outward on both little faces. Stevie had some clinging to her hair.

"Do you mind if I clean them both up? You already have so much to do."

"That I do." Mary shook her head. "Mr. Jon told us what his plans are. For you to stay on as nanny, I mean. I love that baby, but now that I've met you, I hope you take the job. I don't mind the extra work, but there's more to consider. Mr. Jon needs something to bring him out of the shell he's built around himself ever since his wife died. I think you may be just the one to do it. You and your baby."

Beth didn't know what to say. She hadn't considered taking the job to help Jonathan McDuff. Her only reason had been to selfishly keep both girls for herself anyway she could.

Stevie, as usual, put up a fuss when the wet cloth came near her face. When she had her clean, Beth turned to Lexie, unsure of what to expect. But Lexie sat quietly and allowed Beth to wash her face and hands without a murmur. Jonathan came in as she finished.

≈

Jon watched his daughter sitting on Beth's lap while she ran a wash cloth over one of the baby's hands, taking care between each finger as if she didn't want to let go. Lexie looked so completely at home with Beth, a stranger might think she belonged there. A knot formed in the middle of his chest and he stepped forward.

"I think it's about time for Mrs. Garrett to put the girls down for a nap."

Beth looked up at him. A frown touched her face. "I expected to do that myself."

"There's no need." Jon reached for Lexie. The knot in his chest loosened some when she came right to him. "You're our guest this weekend. You may as well take it easy."

"Take it easy?" Beth picked up Stevie. She faced him, each of them holding a baby. "I expected you to understand. Of all people, you should know that I want to spend as much time with Lexie as I can. I've missed a year and a half of her life already. Later on, I may welcome a break now and then. But not today."

Jon's gaze shifted to Stevie. He did know how she felt. That was the problem. He felt the same thing only more. Because he also felt like he was losing Lexie. He shrugged. "Suit yourself."

"Thank you." She started to reach for Lexie, but he pulled back.

"That's okay. I'll walk you up to the nursery."

"Oh, yes. I guess I haven't seen all of the house, have I?"

He smiled at her confusion. "No, but it isn't that big. I'm sure you could have found your way. After all, how many rooms can there be with two baby beds in them?"

"Two?" Beth looked none too pleased.

"Yes, two. I set the second one up last night. You did say later on you might like a break. I assume that means you have decided to stay. Doesn't it?"

"I haven't decided." Beth didn't say more, but Jon could tell by the frown marring her attractive face that she thought plenty. Did she still have it in her head that he planned to steal Stevie away from her?

Jon stepped back at the door of the nursery to allow Beth to enter. He crossed the room to lower Lexie into her bed. He gave her a kiss on the top of her head and said, "Sweet dreams, Lexie girl."

Then he turned to Beth, who stood watching them with Stevie clutched close in her arms. "May I hold her just a moment?"

"I suppose." Beth allowed him to take the baby.

"Dada."

He heard Lexie's call and turned to see her standing in her bed, reaching one hand toward him. Her left thumb had disappeared into her mouth. He glanced at Beth. A smirk sat on her lips. She appeared to be watching to see what he would do.

He strode across the room and scooped Lexie up so that he held both babies, then turned. Beth still watched. He'd show her.

Three long strides and Jon stood in front of Stevie's bed. He drew her close for a kiss, then lowered her over the side into her bed. "Go to sleep, sweetheart, and we'll play when you wake up."

Nary a sound broke the quiet peace of the nursery as he carried Lexie back to her bed. "Night-night, baby. We'll play when you wake up," he repeated so she wouldn't feel left out.

The words were no sooner out of his mouth than a wail sounded from across the room. Garbled words that sounded like "No nap" came from Stevie's bed. He turned to see her clutching the top railing of her bed with one hand and reaching toward him with the other. Tears streamed down her tiny face.

Beth stood to the side with her hand over her mouth. He couldn't be sure, but he thought he heard a snicker from that direction.

"Dada." Lexie wasn't about to let him go to the other baby. From behind, she grabbed his shirt and hung on.

Jon threw both hands out to the side. He knew when he'd been outmaneuvered and when it was time to let a superior negotiator take over. To the tune of Stevie's wail and Lexie's "Dada" repeated over and over with a tug on his shirt each time, Jon appealed to Beth.

"Can you do something here?"

She broke out in laughter. At first he saw nothing funny about the situation, until he looked at it from her point of view. Then a smile pushed his lips up at the corners, and he chuckled.

"Please?" He added, "I'll even help with one of them if you'd like."

Beth shook her head. "If I can't handle two little girls at naptime, I don't need the job taking care of them. Please, just shake yourself free from Lexie and leave me alone with them for a few minutes."

Jon did as she requested, although he didn't see how she could handle it any better than he had. He'd check back in a few minutes, after she'd had time to realize they weren't going to sleep. Then he'd lend a hand.

Twenty minutes later, Jon tiptoed down the carpeted hall toward the nursery. Just outside the door, he heard the sweet sound of a woman singing a lullaby. No yelling, no crying, no Dada's, just the lilting soprano of Beth's voice. He peeked around the corner of the open door.

Beth sat near Stevie's bed in the swivel rocker with Lexie. He could see that Lexie's left thumb was planted in her mouth just as always when she slept. Her eyes were closed, her head snuggled close in the crook of Beth's left arm. Beth's right arm disappeared through the upright spindles of Stevie's bed. He shifted a few inches for a better view. Stevie lay on her tummy with her eyes closed. Beth gently patted her back while she rocked Lexie.

The familiar melody Beth sang caught his attention. "Bye, Baby Bunting, Daddy's gone a-hunting. . ."

Was he the daddy in her song? Or did she think of her deceased husband when she sang? Something akin to jealousy stung his heart as he stood listening. She didn't need his help. Had he made a mistake in bringing Beth to his home? Would she steal Lexie from him?

seven

"She was just about a year old then, wasn't she, Mom?"

Beth listened to Jon's father relate another Lexie tale as his wife nodded her agreement.

"Yes, sir, Robbie and Lexie are quite a pair when you get them together. He got the jelly out and she made short work of it. Her face and hands were purple globs of grape jelly. Well, here, I think there's a picture of her in here somewhere."

Beth laughed at the picture of a younger Lexie caught in the act. Sitting on the kitchen floor beside her young cousin, Robbie, with her hand stuck inside a very messy jelly jar, she looked up at the camera with the innocence of a baby. Ray McDuff was right. She had covered her face and arms to the elbows in globs of jelly. Robbie appeared to be only slightly neater.

Beth had been laughing nonstop, it seemed, since the McDuffs' arrival with picture albums full of their grandson and Lexie, too. But then, Lexie was their granddaughter, wasn't she? Less than one day, and Beth already thought of Lexie as her daughter, which, of course, she was. Beth knew if she thought too much about the situation, she could very easily become confused and frustrated.

She turned then to find Jon's gaze on her. Something in the depths of his dark brown eyes unsettled her. Why did just being in the same room with him set her on edge while every other member of his family seemed so delightful?

Cecelia and her husband, Robert, along with their son, Robbie, had been the first to arrive. Then Jon's younger brother and his wife, Bradley and Donna McDuff, came followed closely by the elder McDuffs. Everyone had welcomed Beth, making her feel like a member of the family. And they had made over Stevie until the child became almost hyper. Beth had never seen her quite so animated. It was almost as if she sensed the importance of the evening and the people surrounding her.

One thing Beth now knew. Lexie had the love of every person there, and the discovery that she was not their own flesh and blood had done nothing to discourage that love. If anything, they loved her even more because now they had Stevie to add to their family circle.

"Ma-maw."

Beth turned at the sound of Stevie's new word. She had taken an instant liking to Jon's mother. Now she stood in front of the older woman, a children's book in her hand, patting her grandmother on the knee.

"Wead." She grinned and her dimple flashed.

"Read you a book?" Her grandmother picked Stevie up and settled her on her lap. "Let's see what you've got here. *Little Red Riding Hood.* Do you think Robbie and Lexie might like to hear this story, too?" She smiled at Robbie when he dropped the toy cars he had been playing with in the corner of the room and came to her. She slipped her arm around him, drawing him to her side, then glanced across the room where Lexie sat curled up on Jon's lap.

"Come on, Lexie." Marion McDuff leaned forward and held an inviting hand out toward Lexie.

Jon turned from his conversation with his brother and nudged his daughter forward. "Grandma wants to read you a story, Lexie."

"They are both so cute," Cecelia confided in Beth just before she gave her hand a quick squeeze. "I'm so glad you decided to come and bring her. We didn't know what we were missing. She looks enough like Lexie to be her sister for real."

Beth smiled at her. "Yes, she does. I guess that's why we didn't discover the switch any sooner."

She watched them urge Lexie to join Stevie on her grandmother's lap and wondered if Lexie might be a tad jealous of another baby taking over her grandmother. All evening, she had been quiet compared to Stevie. After Beth had gotten her up from her nap, just minutes before the family arrived, she had not pushed herself toward Lexie, preferring to allow Lexie to come to her when she was ready. But mostly Lexie had stayed close to Jon, and often Beth had seen her thumb in her mouth.

Beth knew that thumb sucking did not necessarily mean there was a lack in the child's life. Some babies seemed to need the comfort the additional sucking provided while others didn't. Still, she couldn't help wondering if Lexie sucked her thumb because she had been deprived of a mother. If for no other reason than that alone, Beth knew she would accept Jon's offer to care for the two babies together. No longer would her daughter be motherless.

After listening to *Little Red Riding Hood*, Stevie scrambled down and grabbed another book, again demanding that her grandmother "wead" to her. Lexie sat complacently in the circle of her grandmother's arm watching Stevie bring book after book to be read. The only time Stevie sat quietly was during the reading.

Beth noticed Jon kept the conversation with his brother going even as he watched Stevie with what she interpreted as a gleam of pride. Strangely enough, after the warm welcome and acceptance his family had given her, Beth didn't feel so threatened by Jon. She felt as if she had made friends with his family.

Finally, Stevie had been read to enough. She scooted off her grandmother's lap and found Robbie's abandoned cars. Beth watched the three-year-old run across the room to defend his property and was surprised when he knelt beside her and began to play with her.

Beth turned to Cecelia. "I thought there would be a fight over the cars, but your son is a generous little boy."

Cecelia smiled. "Most of the time he is. I think Stevie is just another Lexie to him. We'll have to get together sometime and take the kids to the park."

Beth smiled. "That sounds like fun."

"Then you are staying, aren't you?"

Beth smiled at the eager expression on Cecelia's face. She nodded. "Did you honestly think I could walk away after I met Lexie?"

"Does Jon know?"

"I haven't told him, but I think he suspects. Why wouldn't he? He knew I'd fall in love with her the minute I saw her. What he didn't know is that I loved her already. She's my baby, Cecelia, and I've been cheated out of so much. I'm just thankful that I have the opportunity to be a part of her life while she's so young."

Cecelia patted Beth's hand. "I'm glad. Lexie needs a mama."

❧

Jon closed the door after the last of his departing family and held Lexie close. Beth stood nearby with Stevie. Mary made a quick sweep through the family room, picking up forgotten cups and straightening cushions.

It had been good having his family there. Beth seemed to fit in especially with Cecelia. His dad said he liked her fine. Jon told himself he was glad. If she was going to move into the house and care for the girls, she would have to get along with everyone. Life would be easier if they liked her.

He nuzzled Lexie's neck, delighting in her soft giggles. She threw her little arms around him and gave him a hug. They had been a twosome from the time she was born. No woman coming into his house could change that.

"Time for bed, Lexie girl." He turned to Beth. "Lexie and I always spend time together at bedtime. I give her a bath and get her ready for bed, then I read her a story."

He didn't realize how excluding his words had sounded until he saw the hurt spring to Beth's eyes. Without thinking the offer through, he said, "Maybe the girls would like to take a bath together. If you want, you can join us."

Beth looked at Lexie and a faint smile touched her lips. She nodded. "Yes, I'd like that very much."

The bathroom upstairs was large with plenty of room for two adults to kneel in front of the tub without getting in each other's way. Jon filled the tub while Beth got first Lexie, then Stevie ready for their baths. When she lowered Stevie into the water to join Lexie, she stepped back.

"Stevie likes to splash." The words were no sooner out of Beth's mouth than Stevie hit the water with both hands and giggled.

Jon had no time to get out of the way. A wave of water hit him full in the chest and face as he fell backward on the floor. He gasped and grabbed one of the towels he had placed to the side in readiness for the girls.

As he wiped his face, he heard Beth scold the baby. "No, Stevie, we don't splash. Here, use the washcloth to wash your face."

He looked up at Beth, and she turned toward him where he lay sprawled across the floor, her hand extended. "Do you need help getting up?" The corners of her lips twitched.

He frowned. "Did you teach her that?"

Laughter burst from Beth. She shook her head. "No one has to teach Stevie things like that."

Jon began to laugh until he glanced at the little girls in the tub. He scrambled to an upright position.

"Oh, no."

"What?" Beth swung around to look, her laughter gone.

"She's got Lexie doing it."

Beth was practically leaning over the tub when Lexie hit the water just as hard as Stevie had. Both little girls squealed as the water flew. Only this time Beth got soaked. Hair, face, and blouse dripped. She turned toward Jon, holding her blouse out with both hands, her face the image of shock. Jon handed her the other towel.

Beth buried her face in the towel and Jon chuckled. She looked up with a glare. He laughed. She hugged the towel to her and looked at him. A smile tugged at her lips. The next sound he heard was her laughter. Together they laughed while their baby daughters watched and, he imagined, wondered what was so funny. When Stevie started bouncing in the tub, Jon let the water out.

"I think you've had enough excitement for one evening, young lady." He grabbed a couple more towels from the shelf and handed one to Beth.

"I'm taking this galloping pony before the bathroom floods. You can get Lexie." He didn't wait for her response, but took a dripping baby from the tub and wrapped her in the towel. Stevie looked up at him as if she were trying to figure out who he was and what he might be going to do with her next. He turned her so that she sat on his arm and headed for the door.

"Let's get a diaper and a nightgown on you, okay?" Stevie continued to watch him as he carried her across the hall and into the nursery. He leaned down and kissed her on the cheek and was rewarded with a smile.

"Are you always this feisty? A lot like your old dad, aren't you?" He continued to talk to her as he slipped a diaper under her and fastened it. Next came the nightgown, but he realized he didn't know where Stevie's clothes were. He turned to ask Beth and saw that she hadn't come into the nursery yet.

She stood just outside the door in the hall talking to Mrs.

Garrett. Lexie seemed content to be held close in her arms while the women talked.

Jon waited for a break in their conversation and called, "Beth, can you tell me where Stevie's nightgown is?"

He heard her say, "Excuse me, Mary. It sounds like I'm needed in the nursery."

Beth, still carrying Lexie wrapped in a towel, walked past him to the door that connected the nursery with her room. "It hasn't been unpacked yet."

Within seconds, she came back with the nightgown. Her eyes widened as she looked at Stevie. Jon looked, too, but couldn't see anything wrong.

"You've diapered her?" The inflection in her voice was a cross between question and exclamation.

"Of course. Did you expect me to leave her wrapped in the towel?"

Pink touched Beth's cheeks and she nodded. "Actually, yes. I never thought much about it, but I guess I assumed that men. . .I mean I never knew a man who would. . ."

Jon smiled at her confusion. He'd changed more diapers since he brought Lexie home from the hospital than he'd ever want to count. It wasn't that hard.

"A lot of men change diapers, Mrs. Carter."

"Beth."

"Excuse me?"

"You called me 'Beth' earlier—when you couldn't find Stevie's nightgown. Mrs. Carter sounds so formal if I'm going to be here all the time."

Jon smiled. He felt as if he had been holding his breath since a week ago Thursday night, when he first approached Beth about the job as nanny. He'd been so afraid she would turn him down, and he would lose Stevie. As the tension drained from his body, he nodded and stuck out his hand. "I'm glad to hear you'll be joining us on a permanent basis, Beth."

"Oh, my. I did say that, didn't I?" Beth blushed again and Jon laughed.

He shook her hand, noticing how small and delicate it was. "Yes, you did, so don't even think about trying to back out now."

She kissed the droopy-eyed Lexie in her arms and said, "Don't worry. I couldn't if I wanted to, after meeting my baby."

Her baby? Jon mentally shrugged. Somehow he no longer felt threatened by Lexie's birth mother.

"In that case, we'd better get these girls ready for bed so I can read a story before they go to sleep."

Jon sat in the rocker with a baby snuggled in each arm, and nothing had ever felt more right. He kept the chair moving in a steady rhythm while he read *Beddy Bye Bear.*

He closed the book and looked across the room where Beth sat listening.

"I've never put two to bed before. Would you like to take one so I can get up?"

When Beth smiled, he realized she was even prettier than he had thought. She took Stevie and carried her to her bed. Jon gave Lexie a kiss on the cheek before lowering her into her baby bed and covering her with a quilt.

Jon and Beth passed each other in the middle of the room on their way to say good night to their other child. Jon gave Stevie a kiss, then headed for the door leading to the hall.

He paused with his hand on the door handle. "Please, don't feel that you have to get up at any certain time in the morning."

Beth turned the lights down, using the switch located beside the door to her room. She gave a short laugh. "From that remark, I'd say you haven't been the one to get up with Lexie. Unless Stevie wore herself out today, I'll be up around six in the morning, just as usual."

Jon grinned. "Guilty as charged. I put Lexie to bed, but

Mrs. Garrett gets her up."

Beth nodded toward her room. "This was Mary's room until today, wasn't it?"

"No, actually, it wasn't." Jon paused, wondering if he should tell her the truth, then decided it wouldn't make any difference. "It was my room. Good night, Beth."

Jon chuckled at Beth's surprised expression and pulled the door closed. He whistled as he clomped down the stairs two at a time to the lower floor and his new bedroom just off his den. He always enjoyed the time spent with Lexie, but tonight had been special. He touched his still damp shirt and chuckled. His mom was right. Stevie was a galloping pony. Lexie had caught on awfully quick to her antics, too. That shocked look on Beth's face was one thing about this weekend he'd never forget. He hadn't had so much fun in a long time. Yes, sir, bringing Stevie into his house was the best move he'd ever made.

eight

Beth left Lexie with a promise that as soon as she could tell the kids in her day care good-bye, she would be back. Two minutes after Jon's SUV backed out of her driveway in Bolivar on Sunday afternoon, Beth picked up the phone and punched in Lori's number. When Lori answered, Beth's first words were, "I'm home."

"Good. Are you comfy?"

Beth laughed. "Yes, why?"

"Because I'm curled up on the sofa waiting to hear about your weekend and I don't want you to leave anything out. Wait, where's Stevie? Is she going to interrupt this?"

"No." Beth smiled. "Stevie was asleep when we got here, so we put her to bed."

"We? What's all this 'we' talk? Is Mr. McDuff still there?"

"Of course not. I wouldn't be calling if he was. I just said we because he trailed along when I put her down. He wanted to give her a kiss before he left, that's all."

"Hmm, it's almost one-thirty. You're home before I expected. I assume that means you didn't go to church this morning."

"No, we didn't. I started to, but then I panicked. Lori, you tell me. What would it have looked like for a single dad to suddenly bring a woman and another child to church? Can you imagine the ideas the church family would get from that?"

"Yeah, I see what you mean. So what will you do when you move up there? And don't even try to deny it, Beth. I know you're leaving."

"I'll go to a different church."

"Then you really are moving." Lori's voice sounded flat—matter of fact.

"You knew from the start that I would." Beth slipped her shoes off and wiggled her toes in the carpet. "How could I not? Lexie is my baby. She looks so much like Steven, yet she looks like me, too. It's strange. I can't explain it, but she and Stevie look enough alike to be sisters, yet they are so different."

Beth spent the next several minutes describing her weekend and Lexie. Finally, Lori stopped her by asking, "So, what is Lexie's daddy like? Are you going to be able to get along with your new boss?"

"Jon?" Beth laughed. "For a guy who started out as the enemy, he really isn't that bad."

"No, I guess he isn't if you are already calling him by his first name."

"Oh, Lori." Beth couldn't seem to keep from laughing. "He is so natural with the girls. You should see him in action. Let's face it. A man who changes diapers without cringing can't be all bad."

"He drives a luxury SUV, lives in a mansion, has a house-keeper, and changes diapers? Take my advice and hang on to that man, Beth."

Beth couldn't help but laugh at Lori's silliness. By society's standards, Jonathan McDuff would be considered a wonderful catch. But years earlier, Steven had won her heart. She thought of Jonathan's dark good looks and gentlemanly manners. Then she thought of his obvious love for both of her tiny daughters and she wondered. Had Steven taken her heart to the grave? For more than two years she had thought so. Now she wasn't so sure.

The next day, Beth told each of the parents as they dropped off their children that she would be closing her day care in two weeks. On the ride home from Kansas City, she and Jon had agreed to keep quiet about their babies being switched at birth in an effort to keep the media away. Jon said by not going to court, it was possible that they could keep the story quiet. So she told her day-care parents that she would be moving out of town and nothing more. Most begged her to reconsider, saying they couldn't get along without her.

Debbie's mother summed it up for all of them when she said, "Your day care has been the best I've ever used. Debbie loves to come, yet she's always happy to see me when I pick her up. I know I won't find anyone half as good if I look this town over. We will miss you and Stevie, and I won't be a bit mad if you change your mind at the last minute and stay."

But Beth knew she wouldn't change her mind. Instead, the two weeks she had thought would pass so quickly seemed to take forever. Several children left before the two weeks were over as their parents found other care.

Beth made arrangements with an auctioneer to have her household furnishings and day-care equipment auctioned off under Lori's supervision after she was gone. The final week before she closed her day care, she spent special time with each child that remained. Then Friday evening, she packed personal belongings for her and Stevie while Lori looked on.

"How am I going to get along without you, Beth? First Ron and now you." Lori sat on the bed and watched Beth empty her closet into a suitcase.

Beth stopped and looked at her friend. "Ron ran out on you for no reason. I'm not doing that. I want you to come and visit me."

"Will your boss allow visitors?" The sparkle in Lori's eyes told Beth she was teasing.

Beth rolled her eyes upward and shook her head. "I don't think I'm being imprisoned. According to my boss, I will have two days off each week, which, of course, is ludicrous. As if I'm going to want to be away from my babies two whole days a week. But I will take off a few hours to visit with you." She stopped and tilted her head as if she were thinking. Then she smiled. "And if we go away from the house, we can take Lexie and Stevie with us."

Lori laughed. "Why do I believe you would do exactly that? I don't think I've ever seen a more maternal woman than you, Beth."

Beth clicked the suitcase shut. "I think this one's full. Just one more and I should be finished." She double checked the dresser drawers and nodded her head with satisfaction. "Yep, that should do it."

"Careful, girl. If I didn't know better, I'd think the way you're acting that you are anxious to hit the road headin' north."

A smile lifted the corners of Beth's mouth as she glanced toward Lori. "I am."

❧

Early Saturday morning, Beth locked her house and joined Stevie in her well-packed car. She drove across town to Lori's house, pulled into the drive, and, leaving Stevie in the car, ran to the front door. Lori stepped out before she could knock.

Beth held out the key to her house before she noticed Lori's red-rimmed eyes. "I have until the first of May to get out of the house, so if you are going to boss the auction, you'll need my key. Oh, Lori, don't you dare cry. It's a three-hour trip. That's all."

"Three hours or a lifetime, it's all the same." Lori bit her lower lip. "Who's going to keep me company when I miss Ron? Who's going to come crying on my shoulder when life deals them a bad blow? I thrive on feeling needed."

"Yeah, well just sit by the phone, because you are still needed." Beth gave Lori a quick heartfelt hug. "As soon as I can, I'll be giving you a call. You aren't getting rid of us. Not by a long shot."

"You'd better be telling the truth." Lori swiped at the moisture still in her eyes. "And Mr. Tall, Dark, and Handsome had better let you call me as often as you like. If he does anything that you don't like toward you or Stevie, either one, you let me know and I'll be there so fast it'll make his head swim."

Beth laughed even as tears threatened to fill her eyes. "Oh, Lori, you are the best friend I've ever had and the sister I never had. But don't worry. Jon is too much of a gentleman to hurt me and he already adores Stevie."

"If he's so wonderful, why don't you marry him and solve all your problems?" The teasing sparkle came back into Lori's eyes, but Beth sensed that there was more to her question than she let on.

Beth shook her head. "I don't think I could ever marry again. Not even for the girls. Marriage is too sacred to enter into without love. Divorce is too easy. Then where would the girls be?"

Lori grew serious at once. "I know, Beth. All too well. I loved Ron—and still do with all my heart. But obviously he didn't feel the same for me. I can only thank God that we never had children."

Beth didn't know what to say to bring Lori comfort. She knew from experience that it was best to change the subject when Lori began thinking of Ron and the day he walked out, saying he would not be coming home again.

She gave Lori another hug. "I promise I will call. Soon. I've got to go, though. After all, it is a three-hour drive, and Stevie gets restless if the car isn't moving."

Lori followed Beth to the car and gave Stevie hugs and kisses and a new picture book to look at on the trip. She finally stepped back and let Beth go.

☙

The trip was uneventful, but as Beth entered the congestion of the city, her eagerness to see Lexie warred with the few remaining reservations she had about the move. She breathed a prayer of thanks that she could stay on Highway 71 all the way into Grandview and kept to the far right lane as she drove a bit slower than most of the traffic. A few miles farther brought her to the turnoff to the McDuff house.

Jon was not there when she arrived, but Mary helped her unload a couple of suitcases and convinced her that she could get the rest later or let Jon bring it in when he got home. Except Jon didn't come home before Beth put the little girls to bed that night. After she had the babies tucked in, she retreated to her bedroom and used her cell phone to call Lori. She was glad to find that she could use it in the area without roaming. That meant she wouldn't have to change services, which would be one less complication in her life.

Beth had just said her good-byes to Lori when she heard the hall door to the nursery open. She crept to the connecting door in her room and peeked into the dimly lit nursery. Jon stood beside Stevie's bed. He reached toward her and stroked the hair back from her face. Beth watched as he bent to place a soft kiss on her exposed forehead. Then he crossed the room and repeated the caress with Lexie.

Beth started to push her door closed when Jon turned and looked at her. She couldn't see his expression well but knew when he smiled at her.

"Spying on me, huh?" His voice sounded little more than a whisper.

She nodded and spoke just as softly. "I heard the door open."

"I'm glad to see you made it. Sorry I couldn't be here to welcome you. I've been working on a case. Sometimes it gets crazy when we go to court, and this one's been a doozy from the start. Thankfully, I've wrapped it up now, though."

"That's fine. I didn't mind." Even as she said the words, she realized they weren't completely true. She had minded that he wasn't there. But until that moment, she hadn't rec-ognized that the empty, quiet feel to the house was because

Jon wasn't there. Strange that his presence should make so much difference.

"Well, I'm tired." Jon turned toward the door. "I'll see you in the morning. Sleep well."

"Thank you. Good night." Beth spoke to the closing door and turned back into her own room.

෨

Beth woke early the next morning as sunlight danced through the window beside her bed. She loved having a bedroom on the east side of the house. She glanced around the room, trying to imagine it as Jon's room. Although not feminine, the room did not carry Jon's personality, either. A king-size bed occupied the center of one wall. A large mirrored dresser stood against the side wall. The closet was large, giving her plenty of room for her clothing. She especially liked the rocker-recliner that filled one corner. She figured it had been designed to snuggle into with a good book.

Beth poked her head into the nursery to discover two wide-awake girls. Lexie, lying in her bed, scrambled to clutch the top of the rails as Beth stepped into the room. Stevie, already standing, began to jump and call, "Mama."

Lexie looked across the room at Stevie, then reached one hand toward Beth over the top of her prison. Her little face scrunched seconds before the wail that followed. Beth's heart went out to her daughter, and she took a step toward her.

"Mama, me." Stevie's call held her and she turned toward her daughter. Could she go to one first without hurting the other? After a moment of indecision, two more steps carried Beth to Lexie. Beth scooped her up and, before Stevie could complain, she held Stevie close in her arms, too.

Beth wrinkled her nose. "Oh, my. If you two girls aren't soggy. Let's get you cleaned up, then we'll have some breakfast."

Several hours later, the girls had been fed, bathed, and dressed in their Easter Sunday best. Jon volunteered to watch them downstairs while Beth got herself ready upstairs.

Without Stevie's hindrance, Beth showered and dressed in a hurry. She soon walked back down the stairs and entered the family room where, two weeks prior, Jon's family had met her and Stevie. The room appeared larger this morning with only one chair occupied.

Jon looked at Beth over the top of the two little blond heads on his lap, and she imagined his dark brown eyes brightened as they focused on her. He lowered the book he'd been reading, and Stevie scooted off his lap.

She toddled across the room. "Mama."

Beth picked her up and held her close, reveling in the sweetness of her precious baby. She smiled at the picture Jon and Lexie made in the easy chair across the room. Lexie had no desire to leave the security of her daddy's lap. Although she longed for a relationship with her daughter by birth, Beth breathed a prayer of thanks that Lexie had such a loving father.

"I didn't get a chance to talk to you yesterday." Beth had no idea what Jon's reaction would be to her announcement. She figured the best way to find out would be to plunge right in.

"On the way here, I noticed a church that I thought Stevie and I should try out this morning. I hope you don't mind." She gave a nervous laugh. "Actually, it's so close, I could walk if I needed to."

Jon nodded. "Yes, I've visited there on occasion. From what I've seen, it's a good church. I have no objection, although you are welcome to come with Lexie and me if you'd like."

"Thank you, but, no." Beth shook her head. "To be honest with you, I don't want to give the people in your church or anywhere else, for that matter, anything to talk about."

"I understand and respect that." Jon closed the book he still held and lay it aside. "My family has a few traditions. One of them is that on Easter Sunday we meet at my parents for dinner and an egg hunt for the children. It isn't part of your job, but I'd really like for you and Stevie to come, too. Please?"

When Jon sealed his invitation with a dimple-flashing-heart-stopping grin so like Stevie's, Beth would have agreed to almost anything.

She shrugged. "Sure. It sounds like fun."

೩

And it was. After church, Beth met Jon and Mary back at the house. Mary begged off from the dinner, saying she wanted to visit a friend that afternoon. So Jon, Beth, and the girls loaded into Jon's SUV and drove across town to his parents' house, where a barbeque grill was set up in the backyard.

Before they rounded the corner of the house, Beth could smell the aroma of charcoal-broiled steaks cooking, and her stomach growled. She glanced at Jon, thankful that he hadn't heard or was too polite to indicate that he had. She couldn't remember when she'd attended an outdoor barbeque. Obviously, being part of a large family had its rewards.

"Beth, come on over here," Cecelia called out.

With Stevie being passed from one woman to another, Beth relaxed and enjoyed herself. Jon's sister-in-law, Donna, left and soon came back with Lexie. She hugged the little girl and said, "I don't know how you can keep your hands off this little doll."

Whether she meant the remark as criticism or not, Beth took it that way. She looked at Lexie and wished she felt the freedom to keep her by her side always.

She answered Donna. "It's about all I can do to keep a little distance. But I want Lexie's love and acceptance. I don't want to force her in any way. And to be honest, I guess a small part of me is afraid to get too close. I don't know if I could handle losing her now that I've found her."

"Oh, pooh." Cecelia brushed away the serious words. "Don't even think such a thing. You aren't going anywhere and neither is Lexie. My prediction is that you will raise both your daughters and see them marry and give you grandchildren.

Freaky circumstances brought you into our family. But now that you are here, we don't intend to ever let you go."

"Mama, bubbles." Stevie tugged on Beth's skirt.

Beth couldn't have responded to Cecelia if she'd tried and was glad for the interruption. She knelt beside her daughter and accepted the puff of dandelion seeds. "Yes, you found some dandelion bubbles, didn't you?"

"Bubbles?" Donna set Lexie on the ground as she squirmed to get down with Stevie. "How cute."

Beth laughed. "Yes, that's what she calls them."

Lexie grabbed the stem in her hand, causing an uproar from Stevie. Beth pointed to some more dandelions that had sprung up in the otherwise neat yard. "Look, Lexie, can you get some over there?"

Lexie released Stevie's dandelion and toddled away to get her own. She came back with one clutched in her hand, a happy smile lighting her face. "Bubbles."

"Isn't it funny how quickly they catch on to something like that?" Donna laughed.

"Let's have that egg hunt." Jon came and took Stevie and Lexie into the house. Beth overheard him admiring their bubbles and wondered what he thought of Stevie teaching Lexie to call them that.

"I can't wait until Bradley and I have a little one to look for eggs, too." Donna looked wistfully as her husband helped his father hide eggs around the backyard. She shrugged then. "Maybe in a couple of years we will have. But for now we have our Floppsie."

"Floppsie?" Beth couldn't resist asking.

Donna smiled. "Yes, she just had puppies. They are the cutest little things. Both are little balls of fur."

Ray McDuff stuck the last egg in plain view on the seat of the picnic table. He called to Cecelia. "Tell them we're ready now."

Jon came out of the house carrying a baby on each arm. His mother followed with her grandson. Beth felt left out until Jon stood in front of her with a grin.

"Which one do you want?"

Beth didn't need to make the decision as Stevie lunged for her. She followed Jon to the center of the yard, where his mother waited with Robbie. They set the children down and crouched beside them. As soon as their grandfather gave the signal, the adults crowded around the little ones, encouraging them to find eggs.

Jon helped Lexie while Beth helped Stevie until they found themselves in front of the same egg. While they held back, not wanting to give either child the advantage, Stevie reached down and picked up the egg. Her dimple flashed as she held it with both hands toward Beth. Just as Beth reached for it, Stevie turned and gave it to Jon.

"Why, you little stinker." Beth acted as if she were going to grab her little turncoat daughter.

Stevie squealed and ran into Jon's waiting arms. He bent to give her a kiss on the forehead. Then he grabbed her up and sat her on his bent leg to kiss her again.

Beth sensed that something had changed in his actions and wondered until he looked up without a trace of amusement and said, "Stevie has a fever."

nine

"Stevie has a virus?"

"Yes, ma'am." The doctor barely glanced up from his pre-scription pad. "It'll run its course in a couple of days, then she'll be up getting into things again." He handed Beth the prescription he'd just written. "This should help with the fever and those aches that come with it."

"You're sure she'll be all right?" Jon held Stevie close in his arms. He had scarcely left her side since the day before, when he discovered she had a fever.

"Oh, yes, she'll be fine. If her temperature comes up, bathe her with lukewarm water. Unless it goes too high. Then you call me."

As they left the office, Beth looked at Jon. "Are you sure he knows what he's doing?"

"He's a pediatrician. I've always brought Lexie to him. Why?"

She shrugged. "I don't know. He just seemed so unprofes-sional. So laid back. . .so, I don't know. . . ."

"Matter of fact? Unconcerned?" Jon nodded. "Yeah, but maybe there isn't that much to be concerned about. Maybe what she has isn't serious."

"I hope not."

They stopped to get the prescription filled before going home. Beth assumed Jon would go to the office after drop-ping her and Stevie off at the house, but he insisted on carry-ing Stevie upstairs. When he sat in the rocker with Stevie cuddled against his chest, Beth turned and went back down-stairs in search of Lexie. She found Mary watching cartoons on TV while Lexie stood at the coffee table coloring.

When Mary looked up, Beth said, "I hadn't realized that you like cartoons."

Mary smiled. "Oh, yes. I watch at least one every day or so."

Beth laughed. "Stevie has never sat still long enough to get involved in TV. Then, too, I always had the day care, so she wasn't exposed to it much."

Mary stood. "You are to be commended for that. Now, tell me what you found out about Stevie."

"She has a virus. The doctor said she'd be up and around in a couple of days. Jon's with her now."

Mary moved to the door, chuckling. "I wouldn't be surprised if he stays with her until he knows for sure she's going to be all right."

"Oh, no, he will have to go to work, won't he?"

Mary stopped just short of going through the door. "Don't count on getting rid of him too soon." She nodded toward Lexie. "That baby means the world to him. I look for Stevie to find an equal place in his heart."

Beth watched Mary disappear into the dining room. She wasn't sure how she felt about Stevie becoming so important to Jon. She knelt beside Lexie and gave her a quick hug. "May I color with you?"

Lexie looked at Beth over her shoulder. "Uh-uh."

"No? Why not?" Beth picked up a red crayon. "How about if I color the sweater red?"

Lexie scooped up her coloring book and stepped around the corner of the low table to lay it back down. She scribbled several lines through the picture before flipping the page over to color more, ignoring Beth.

Beth sat back on her heels. Jon had taken over Stevie, and Lexie wouldn't let her near. Tears of self-pity stung her eyes.

What had she done? Come to Kansas City to let Jonathan McDuff steal both her girls right out from under her nose?

Well, he wouldn't get away with it. She stood and held out her hands toward Lexie. "Come on, darling. Let's go upstairs and see what Daddy and Stevie are doing."

"Dada?" Lexie's eyes brightened at the name.

Beth felt a weight drop on her heart. Lexie left no doubt as to who owned her affections. The experts said that the first few years of a child's life set the pattern for the rest of his life. Did that mean she had already lost Lexie? Was there no room in her little daughter's heart for her mother?

Lexie came to her easily enough and Beth knew why. She wanted to go see her precious dada. Beth carried her up to the nursery, where she met Jon backing out of the door.

He put a finger to his lips. "She's asleep. I gave her the first dose of medicine and she was out like a light."

"Dada." Lexie leaned for Jon.

Jon took her and kissed her on the forehead. Beth knew he was checking for fever. She would have liked to stamp her foot, but instead folded her arms and with a touch of ice to her voice said, "She's fine."

Jon leaned back just a bit to see Lexie better. "Good. I want her to stay that way. What would you say if we moved her bed out of the nursery until Stevie's fever breaks?"

"Where?"

"I don't know. Mary's room or mine." Then as if reading the anger in her voice and eyes, he added, "I'd rather she be as far from the nursery as possible. You'll be busy with Stevie, anyway."

Beth shrugged. "I suppose." She hadn't been busy with Stevie yet. She hadn't given her any medicine and she hadn't put her to sleep. She had held Lexie maybe two minutes, which was just enough time to get her to her daddy. She was the nanny, not to mention the mother, and she couldn't get near the children.

Lexie slept in Mary's room for the next two nights while

Stevie's fever gradually disappeared. Jon popped in and out of the nursery so much, Beth wondered if he didn't trust her to care for her own daughter. About the only time she could be assured of his absence was during the afternoon while both girls took a nap.

Then in spite of Jon's precautions, Lexie came down with the same symptoms Stevie had, and Jon moved her back into the nursery. Beth half-expected him to blame her for Lexie's sickness, but he simply shrugged and said, "I guess I didn't get her moved soon enough. She probably caught the bug when Stevie first got sick."

Beth nodded. "My experience in day care taught me that anything contagious spreads from one child to another almost before you know it's there."

With both girls back in the nursery, Beth became even busier than before keeping Stevie occupied while tending to Lexie's needs. Lexie fussed at the least provocation and refused to take her medicine.

Beth held her in the rocking chair, talking to her, trying to convince her that the clear red liquid tasted good. She held the syringe filled with a teaspoon of medicine ready to squeeze into her little girl's mouth at any moment. "Come on, sweetheart. Stevie likes the medicine and you will, too. Can you open up for—"

She had almost said, "For Mama." That would be a sure way to lose her job if Jon happened along. She glanced toward the door and almost dropped the medicine when she saw him leaning against the doorframe. Had he heard her slipup, and did he know what she hadn't said?

She willed her heart to slow its rapid pounding. "Hi, you startled me. How long have you been there?"

"Long enough." He pushed away and crossed the room to kneel beside her. "Let me help you. Lexie does not take medicine willingly. I always lay her on her back with her head elevated. Once it touches her tongue and she realizes it isn't so terrible, she's fine."

Beth allowed Jon to position Lexie across her lap with her head on her arm. He held the baby's head still with a hand on either side of her face. Then he nodded to Beth. "Go ahead."

Beth pushed the tip of the syringe between Lexie's lips, and she opened her mouth to cry. Just as Jon had said, when she squeezed a few drops on her tongue, the crying stopped and she swallowed. Beth quickly emptied the rest of the teaspoon into Lexie's mouth.

"Wow." Beth looked at Jon and smiled. "You must have done this before."

"Yes, a time or two. I usually have Mrs. Garrett or whoever is handy to help me. Sadly, Lexie doesn't seem to learn that the medicine isn't a bad thing, so each time it's given, we have to go through the same process."

Beth helped Lexie sit up and was surprised when she didn't immediately launch herself at her father. Beth gave her a quick hug and settled back in the chair to rock her. At that moment, Stevie brought a book to Jon and patted his leg.

"Wead."

Jon laughed and Beth's breath caught in her throat. She had always liked the lone dimple beside Stevie's mouth, but on Jon, it had a devastating effect on her heart. An effect she had no interest in pursuing.

His amused gaze met hers over Lexie's head and something in his look changed as he focused on her eyes and then her mouth. For the longest three seconds of her life, Beth stared at Jon until he blinked and smiled. Then, as if nothing had happened, he slipped an arm around Stevie and asked, "Is this girl a readaholic or what?"

He took the book and tickled Stevie until she giggled and struggled to get away. Beth watched with a sad smile. This was what Stevie had missed by not having a father. Jon was good for her. She held Lexie close and felt her baby snuggle even deeper into her arms as she kept the rocker going. Lexie needed a mother just as much as Stevie needed a father. They had both missed so much. But would their temporary arrangement heal the losses their babies had suffered or cause an even greater loss at some point later in their lives? Beth couldn't help wondering what would happen when her services as nanny were no longer needed in the McDuff family.

She leaned her head back against the chair and closed her eyes as Jon sat on the floor to read with Stevie on his lap. While Jon and Stevie were occupied, Beth breathed a silent prayer for strength and direction. How could she stand to lose her daughter again, now that she had held her and loved her?

"Trust in the Lord with all thine heart, and lean not unto thine own understanding; in all your ways acknowledge Him, and He shall direct your paths."

Scripture she had known from childhood came to her mind. As she pondered the words, she realized that God did not want her questioning His plan for her. If she put her trust in Him and acknowledged His Lordship in her life, she had nothing to worry about. He would direct her paths and, as her heavenly Father, He would lead her only into good.

She looked down at Lexie and saw that she was asleep. Did all mothers think that their child was beautiful far beyond that of other children? She glanced at Stevie and smiled. Obviously the delusion had nothing to do with giving birth. Stevie and Lexie were equally beautiful in her eyes.

Jon closed the book and, with Stevie still on his lap, looked at Lexie, then up at Beth. "I see our patient is asleep. Do you want me to put her to bed?"

Beth started to say no but changed her mind. She nodded. "Yes, if you don't mind."

"Not at all." Jon let Stevie go and hopped up. He picked Lexie up with a gentleness that Beth did not miss. When he turned from the baby bed, he returned to his spot on the floor and watched Stevie sort through a shelf of books. When she made her selection and brought a second book to him, he picked up the first she had discarded on the floor and handed it to her.

"Let's put this book back before we read another."

She shoved the new book at him. "Wead."

He took the book and again handed her the first one. "Okay, I'll read when you put this one up."

Stevie took the book and ran across the room to poke it at the shelf of books. Beth watched Jon grin at her effort, and she sighed. Stevie seemed to be bonding with Jon. She knew she should be glad, but she wasn't. Not really. And she knew self-ishness and jealousy were wrong.

"Why don't you take a break?" Jon asked. "You've been cooped up in here for three days and probably will be for two more. Go shopping or do something fun for yourself. You need the time away."

Beth shook her head. "No, I'm fine."

Jon shrugged. "Maybe you are and maybe you aren't. But wouldn't you be a better mother if you had some time to yourself once in a while?"

"Do you have a problem with my work?" Beth felt the sting of his words even when she knew he hadn't meant criticism by them.

Jon's eyebrows lifted. "Are you kidding? The girls are clean, well fed, and happy. You treat them both the same. I don't think I've ever seen any child get as much loving attention as you give both of these babies. I don't know how you do it especially when one or the other has been sick and fussy ever since you've been here. That's why I think you need a break. Take a couple of hours at least to do something fun just for yourself. Take the rest of today and tomorrow if you want."

Beth laughed at the thought of her leaving Lexie for so

long while she was sick. She shook her head. "You know I won't do that."

"Then just take a few hours. Stevie and I can read that long, can't we, Stevie?"

Stevie plopped on Jon's lap and grinned. "Wead. Book."

Beth smiled. "I know Stevie can. The question is, can you?"

Jon laughed. "If not, I'll fake it."

"All right." Beth headed toward her bedroom. "I'll go."

She closed the bedroom door and reached for her purse lying on the dresser. Where would she go? What would she do? She didn't want to go shopping. Then she had an idea. She dropped her purse back in place and went out the door to the hall.

Mary wasn't hard to find. When Beth presented her plan, Mary gladly let her have the run of the kitchen. Beth loved to cook and had missed making snacks for the children in her day care. She washed her hands as she debated with herself whether to make a nutritious snack or let herself go with chocolate chip cookies.

As soon as she saw Mary's supplies, she decided on the cookies. An hour later, Beth pulled her last batch of cookies from the oven. She scraped the cookies onto a platter already heaped and running over. She washed the cookie sheet and wiped the counter. Mary's kitchen looked as good as new, except for all the cookies on the table. Three platters held more cookies than the entire McDuff family could eat in a week.

Beth took a clean plate from the cabinet and selected three oatmeal-raisin cookies, three chocolate chip cookies, and three peanut butter cookies. She lifted her eyes to the ceiling and laughed. Stevie couldn't eat three cookies, she probably couldn't eat three cookies, and Jon probably wouldn't want to.

"Oh, well." She spoke aloud. "It's Jon's fault I did this so he'd better eat his share."

She poured milk into a sippy cup and two glasses, placed everything on a tray, and headed upstairs. She met Mary on the stairs coming down. When Mary eyed her snack, Beth smiled.

"As you can see, I got carried away. Please help yourself to as many cookies as you want."

Mary nodded. "I believe I'm ready for a cookie break. Those sure do smell good."

"Thank you." Beth went on to the nursery, hoping that Jon would think the same.

He looked up when she entered the room. "Back so soon?"

"I didn't go anywhere." Beth set the tray on a low table in the corner. She pulled out one of the tiny chairs. "Come on, Stevie. Snack time."

Stevie scrambled to the table, and Beth handed her a cookie and her sippy cup. Jon joined them, standing next to Beth. He reached for a cookie and took a bite.

"M-m-m, this is good." He reached for another. "You were supposed to get away and do something fun, but I'm not complaining. I hope you made enough."

Beth giggled. "Wait until you see your kitchen table."

❧

Jon lay back on the quilt Beth had spread over the grass and relaxed. Warm sunshine touched his arm and neck, making him sleepy. He could hear one bird calling to another. He closed his eyes to listen. He heard children's voices in the distance as they played some game. Two people walked past, talking. A wet tongue slurped across his cheek.

He sat up, wiping the side of his face. "Yuck. I wasn't expecting that."

Stevie giggled and clapped her hands. Lexie followed her lead. Beth laughed. The guilty puppy placed both paws on Jon's leg and tried to climb into his lap.

Jon pushed him away. "Stop that. You've done enough

bonding with me for one day. Go play with the girls."

Stevie grabbed the puppy. "Mine goggy."

Lexie reached a tentative hand out and touched the puppy's head. She laughed, jerking her hand back. "Goggy."

Jon took Lexie's hand and helped her pet the puppy. The small animal squirmed in Stevie's arms until he broke free and both girls squealed. The puppy, wriggling from one end to the other, bounced between the babies, causing giggles and squeals.

Jon shared an amused look with Beth as she sat back watching them. Bringing his brother's puppy on their outing to the park had been a good idea. After being cooped up in the house all week, the girls and Beth needed to be out in the sunshine and fresh air.

He watched Beth disengage Stevie's arms from the puppy's neck and marveled at her loving patience with both girls. He tried to visualize Sharolyn in her place and couldn't. Sharolyn hadn't wanted a baby. Beth wanted both babies.

"Oh, how cute!" An older couple stepped close and watched the babies and puppy for a moment. The woman's lined face wore a big smile. "Twins. One baby is adorable, but when you have twins, you triple your fun. And both of yours are just as cute as they can be."

Beth smiled and thanked the woman. Jon could do little more than nod. Why hadn't he thought how much like a family he and Beth and the girls would appear to others? This was why Beth wouldn't attend his church. He should have known better.

He watched Beth smile and talk to the couple as they admired the babies. How soon would it take Beth to decide marriage was the only way out of their unique relationship? A band of fear tightened around his chest. Never would he marry and again live in bondage to a woman who cared nothing for him. He could not trust his wife; how could he trust

Beth? Two different women with two different purposes, yet he could trust neither. Sharolyn had put her life at risk to destroy their child. Beth would do what she could to take both his daughters from him. He realized that now.

As soon as the couple moved away, Jon grabbed the puppy and put him in the pet carrier. Without explanation for his changed mood, he said, "It's getting late. The girls need to calm down before supper."

Beth gave him a look that clearly said she thought he had just lost what little intelligence he possessed, then she began gathering toys and a baby. Without a word, she took her load to the SUV. Jon followed with the remaining baby and the puppy. When they had babies and puppy buckled into the vehicle, Jon ran back for the quilt, knowing he was in for a quiet ride home and thankful for it. His mind churned with unanswered questions and feelings that needed to be worked through.

ten

Jon helped Beth take the girls into the house and deposit them in the family room. He stepped to the door saying, "I'll take the puppy back to Brad's now. Please, tell Mrs. Garrett I won't be here for dinner."

Beth nodded and watched him walk away. She ran over the events of the afternoon and could think of nothing that might have caused him to be angry with her. Had she said something that triggered a memory or that he might have taken the wrong way? She decided the problem wasn't hers and turned to the girls.

She and Mary ate Sunday dinner with the girls. Mary seemed unconcerned by Jon's absence, but Beth's gaze continually wandered to the empty chair at the head of the table. Even with Mary's friendly chatter and the babies' antics, Beth could not keep her mind from Jon. While Mary cleaned up from their meal, Beth took the girls upstairs.

Jon's nightly routine with Lexie had become hers and Stevie's, as well. Beth knew she wasn't the only one missing Jon when she put Lexie in the tub and large blue eyes looked at her questioningly.

"Dada?"

Stevie hit the water causing a splash and mimicked Lexie. "Dada!"

As she dodged the water, Beth's heart dropped. "No, Stevie." She spoke harsher than normal. "We don't splash water."

Stevie looked at her with a solemn face. "Dada bye-bye."

"No." Beth started to say, "He isn't your dada," but stopped.

97

Of course he was Stevie's daddy. Tears stung her eyes and she wiped them away. She couldn't fight the inevitable. Stevie would learn to call Jon "Daddy." It was only right that she should if they were going to live in the same house. She should never have brought Stevie here in the first place. She should have known it would cause more problems than she could handle.

Beth finished the girls' baths and put them to bed, then went into her own room, leaving the door ajar. She fell across the bed and thought of Jon and how he played with the babies. His love for both was evident in everything he did and said.

Two short weeks in the McDuff family home and she couldn't love Lexie any more than she did at that moment. Probably Jon felt the same for Stevie.

As she thought about their situation, Beth longed for someone to talk to. She had called Lori only once since she'd been in Kansas City other than the first short call to let her know she had arrived safely. She needed to talk to Lori.

Beth reached for the phone on her night table by the bed. Jon had told her to use it freely, yet she still hesitated. She held the cordless receiver in her hand and stared at it a moment before pushing the first number. After that, her finger couldn't push the other buttons fast enough.

"Hello?"

"Lori, it's Beth." Hot tears stung her eyes and she dabbed at them with her shirt. Thankfully, Lori couldn't see her.

They talked for a few minutes, catching up on the progress of Beth's sale.

"The auction is scheduled for this Saturday. I wish you could come down for it and bring Stevie. I really miss you guys."

"I know. Stevie still thinks we should go see her aunt Lori sometimes." Beth's breath caught in her throat. She hadn't realized how much she missed her life in Bolivar until that moment.

"What's wrong, Beth? Remember who you are talking to. I can hear the tears in your voice. Is that guy giving you a hard time?"

Beth gave a short laugh. "No, Jon is fine. He couldn't be nicer."

"Hmmm. That means you like him. The question is, how much do you like him?"

"Oh, Lori." Beth felt a flush move to the roots of her hair. She started to deny Lori's implication, then shook her head. What was the use? She needed to tell someone.

"The answer to that is, he's wonderful with the babies. He loves Stevie already as much as I love Lexie. He's a gentleman toward me and I have free run of the place. I like him very much, Lori. More than I should, considering the fact that he has no feelings one way or another toward me. Does that satisfy your curiosity?"

"Not completely since we're talking *like* instead of love here. How long until you two fall in love and get married? You know that would take care of your problem with the children, don't you?"

Beth sat on her bed in stunned silence. How had the conversation taken this turn? She shook her head as if to clear it. "I won't deny thinking along those lines, but you know that's a fantasy, don't you? Life isn't ordered into such neat fairy tale stories. Besides, I still love Steven and probably always will. There's no room in my heart for another man. I'm sure Jon feels the same way about his wife."

"It's still early, Beth. Just give it some time."

Beth decided to ignore Lori's advice. "I've been asked out. Would you like to hear about that?"

"On a date?" The excitement in Lori's voice carried across the line. "You never date. This must be good."

Beth laughed, shoving her hair behind her ear. "Maybe I'm getting daring up here in the city. He attends the same church I do. The adult singles' Sunday school class is holding a banquet and he asked if I'd go with him."

"Well, are you going?"

"I don't know. I haven't decided."

&a.

Across town, at the same park they had been to earlier, Jon sat by the lake and watched the gentle lap of water against the bank. After dropping the puppy off at his brother's, he stopped at a fast food drive-in and ordered the greasiest hamburger and fries they had. At least they felt greasy now on his stomach.

Or was it the image of Beth playing with their babies that weighed on him so heavily? He watched sunlit waves shimmer across the water. Earlier, the sun touching Beth's dark hair had brought out burnished copper highlights. Like flecks of fire, they danced through her long wavy hair, and he'd wanted to catch some just to hold in his hand.

He gave an impatient shrug and blinked his eyes to clear Beth's image from his mind. What was the matter with him? He didn't need any more complications in his life. He brought memories of Sharolyn to his mind so he wouldn't have to think of Beth.

Sharolyn had thrown a fit the day she discovered she was pregnant. At first he hadn't caught on to her anger. He had been so thrilled with the prospect of becoming a father. Then her words penetrated his happiness.

"I want an abortion, Jonathan." She glared at him. "This is your fault. I told you from the start I didn't want children and I won't have this one."

How anyone could make the word *children* sound like a dirty word, he didn't know. But Sharolyn had. She then ranted on about getting fat and ugly. When she wouldn't stop, he grabbed her and forced her to listen to him.

He spoke with deadly quiet. His voice was cold and hard. "You will not get an abortion. If you do anything at all to kill my child, I'll take you to court. I'm an attorney, Sharolyn. My dad and my sister are attorneys. We'll wipe the ground with you, then leave you there to rot. You'll find yourself divorced with barely enough alimony to keep you off the streets."

His threat had worked for several months while Sharolyn's anger boiled just below the surface of the calm face she displayed. As the baby became evident, she again approached him. When he denied her wish to end the life within her, he saw the hatred in her eyes and knew that his marriage was a joke. Sharolyn didn't love him and never had. Sharolyn loved his money. She feared losing her security of credit cards and ready cash, and on that slender thread hung the life of his child.

Again he reminded her that she would be cut off with barely enough to survive if anything happened to the baby. And again she backed off. Until the night she ran out of the house. The night Stevie was born and Sharolyn died.

A cool breeze stirred the surface of the water before him. Jon zipped his jacket and leaned back with one elbow on the ground.

As he stared at the rippling water, Beth's sweet image returned to drive away the ghosts of his past. She had enjoyed their outing, he was sure. She seemed to dote on anything the girls did. When Stevie claimed the puppy as hers and when Lexie overcame her shyness toward the wiggling bundle of fur, Beth's eyes had shone with maternal pride.

How could two women be so different? Sharolyn's beauty held no depth, her veins flowed with ice water, and her selfish greed had known no limit. Beth portrayed a soft feminine appearance that, while not stunningly beautiful, was certainly pleasing to the eye. Yet beauty was not important to Jon.

What he admired most in Beth was her patience and love for their babies and her obvious dedication to the Lord.

Images of their outing that afternoon and other incidences over the past two weeks played through his mind as thoughts of Sharolyn faded into the past. Could things be different a second time with a different woman? Could God have sent Beth to him for a purpose?

No. He could not let down his guard in a moment of weakness.

He had stepped outside the will of God when he married Sharolyn. Except two be in agreement, how can they walk together? He and Sharolyn had never agreed on anything.

A chill moved through his body where he lay on the cold, damp ground. The sun had long since gone down and left the park shrouded in a gray blanket. Jon sat up and buried his face in his hands. He could never marry again. He could never trust another woman. Sharolyn had taught him that.

He stood and moved with leaden feet toward his SUV. Although Beth seemed to be a sweet, innocent woman, he knew she had one goal in life. She wanted to take both children as her own. She would probably marry him in a minute to gain custody of Lexie. But he would not allow another woman to manipulate him into a loveless marriage.

Jon inserted his key and started the SUV. As he turned toward home, he promised himself that he would keep Beth at arm's length if it took every ounce of willpower he had.

❧

Beth heard Jon come into the nursery to check on the babies. She had long since ended her phone visit with Lori and now sat reading her Bible. If Jon noticed that her light was still on, there was no indication. She heard his soft voice tell each of the girls that he loved her and that he would see her the next day. Then she heard the nursery door click as he pulled it closed.

Beth closed her Bible and prepared for bed. Whatever had been eating at Jon was none of her concern. She felt sure that he would return to normal the next day.

But the next day, Jon's normally cheerful greeting changed into a mere nod and a stiff, "Good morning." That evening he took the girls outside to play, making it clear that she was not invited. At bedtime, he asked to be excused from their bath routine, saying he would come up later to read to the girls before they went to bed.

Beth tried to not let his new attitude toward her hurt, but as the week passed and he continued to avoid her, she realized that something was wrong. By Saturday morning, she knew that the friendship she thought they had was nonexistent. She also made the decision that she would tell Jon of the invitation she had received from Bob Macklin to attend the singles' Sunday school banquet at her church. If he had no reasonable objections, she would accept the invitation the next day when she went to church.

While the girls took their afternoon naps, Beth went in search of Jon and found him in his den. She knocked on the open door, waiting until he turned to see her.

"If you don't mind, may I talk to you for a minute?"

He nodded, turning back to some papers on his desk.

She hesitated before saying, "I have been invited to attend a banquet at the church I've been going to."

Jon's head came up and he frowned. "Invited? By a man?"

She nodded. "Yes, Bob Macklin. Our Sunday school singles' class puts it on. I wanted to know if you have any objections to me being gone for a few hours next Saturday evening. I don't believe they will stay late, but someone will need to take my place with the girls."

Jon picked up a pencil and made a notation on the paper in front of him. Beth wondered if he had understood that she was asking for his permission and needed an answer. She started to speak again when he shrugged.

"I told you from the start that you may take off two days each week. To my knowledge, you haven't taken any time since you've been here. Mrs. Garrett and I can take care of the girls. Don't worry about them."

"You don't mind then?" She almost hoped he would say that he couldn't get along without her.

"No, of course not. Go on and have fun. You've been working too much and deserve a break."

Disappointment settled on Beth's heart as she turned toward the door. She remembered to thank him before she left the room and headed toward the nursery.

Lexie was awake, standing in her bed when Beth stepped through the door. Tears stung her eyes as she eased Lexie back down and quickly changed her soggy diaper. When she lifted the baby and gave her a hug, she thought of Jon's unconcerned shrug and a tear traveled down her cheek.

Lexie looked at her with a frown on her tiny face. Then she reached out with her little finger and touched the tear.

"Mama cwy."

"You called me 'Mama.'" Beth felt as if her heart would burst. She held her daughter close and gave freedom to tears of hurt and happiness as they mingled on her cheeks.

❧

Jon sat at his desk and stared through the open doorway where Beth had been only moments before. The pencil in his fingers snapped in two, and he jumped. Releasing the pent-up tension in his arm, he threw the pieces across the room and stood to pace from one end of the room to the other and back again.

How had it happened? At what point had Beth become so important to him? As caretaker for his children—yes. He needed her for that. No question about it. But at the moment, his thoughts of Beth held little resemblance to his thoughts of a nanny.

He recognized the raging jealousy that ate at his heart, and he was disgusted with himself for his weakness. He had determined to stay away from her and had been satisfied that he had accomplished just that. Until now.

Beth had the right to date anyone she wished. Why, then, did he feel as if she had just asked permission to cheat on him?

eleven

Beth dressed for her date, brushed her hair until it shone, then put it up in a roll on the back of her head. One last glance at the mirror and she was satisfied that she would do well enough for a widowed mother of two. She turned from the mirror to stare out the window to the street below.

She wondered what she thought she was doing, going on a date? Bob Macklin was a nice enough man, she supposed. He attended church regularly. He was clean and neat about his appearance and he was reasonably good looking. But, as she thought about it, she wondered if she had accepted his invitation for the sole purpose of getting Jon's attention. Not that it had worked. For the past two weeks, he had ignored her as if their earlier camaraderie had never existed.

She missed Steven so much. If he had not died, she would not be in the position of losing her heart to another man only to have him break it and toss away the pieces. A ragged sigh tore from her lips, and she turned toward the door leading into the nursery. It was time for her to go downstairs.

Mary sat in the rocker watching the two babies play with some toys in the corner of the nursery. She smiled as Beth stepped through the door.

"My, don't you look pretty."

"Thank you." Beth smoothed her hands down the light blue folds of her skirt and returned Mary's smile. "I thought I should tell the girls bye before I go downstairs."

Mary looked toward the girls as Lexie handed a doll to Stevie. "They are becoming fast friends, aren't they?"

"Yes, they are." Beth winced. That was another complication

for her to deal with. With Jon acting so strange toward her now, how long would it be before he asked her to leave? Stevie would never understand being torn away from her sister for, surely, she and Lexie were becoming as close as sisters. Which meant Lexie would be hurt, too.

Beth knelt beside the girls and gave them each a hug and kiss. Stevie showed her the baby doll she held, and Beth had to kiss it, too. When she stood, she wished she could slip back into a pair of jeans and T-shirt and play house with her little ones.

"Don't worry about them. We'll be fine." Mary's voice forced her from the nursery. "To tell the truth, I've missed playing with Lexie since you've been here. We'll have twice as much fun with Stevie."

Beth closed the nursery door behind her and went downstairs, determined to have a good time. She glanced at her watch. It was almost time for Bob to come.

The front door of the house opened into an entry hall separated by a half wall from a small sitting room to the left. Beth assumed that would be a good place to wait for Bob since she could more easily hear when he came to the door.

As she stepped around the corner into the sitting room, she realized that Jon must have had the same idea. He sat in a recliner, hiding behind a newspaper. As she hesitated, he lowered the paper and let his gaze travel from her upswept hairdo to the soles of her two-inch heels.

Although an expression she couldn't read swept across his face, all he said was, "You look nice."

"Thank you." She took another tentative step into the room. "I thought I'd wait for Bob in here since it's close to the door."

"Yes, it is that." Jon lifted the paper again.

"Are you going to stay here?" Beth hoped not.

The paper lowered. "Yes, if you have no objections."

"Well, actually—" The doorbell cut into Beth's objection.

"That must be him now." Jon folded the paper and stood. "Would you like for me to get the door?"

"No!" Horror stricken, Beth looked toward the door, then back at Jon. What did he think he was doing? Even her father had never been so conspicuous when she dated as a teenager. "That's all right. There's no need for you to bother."

"Oh, it's no bother at all." Jon stepped around her and reached for the door.

Beth had no time to think or call out a protest before Jon had invited Bob inside.

Where was the proverbial hole in the floor to swallow her when she needed it? Beth felt heat cover her face as Bob turned a puzzled look her way.

Jon grabbed Bob's hand and pumped. "Hi, I'm Jonathan McDuff. And I assume you are the Bob Macklin that Beth's been talking about?"

Bob nodded but appeared to be speechless. Beth summoned enough strength to move and grab Bob's arm before Jon could do any more damage. Although she didn't think his vigorous handshake would be as dangerous as what he might say next, she didn't intend to stay long enough to find out.

But before she could close the door, Jon caught it and leaned out to call, "Don't worry about our babies, Beth. I'll take good care of them."

Beth almost ran to the car, pulling Bob behind her.

To his credit, Bob remained quiet until he pulled into the church parking lot two blocks down the street. Then he turned off the engine and stared out the windshield of his late-model car. His voice, when he spoke, sounded forced. "Who was that?"

"You mean at the house?"

He looked at her then. "Yes. I knew you had one daughter. I thought you were widowed."

Beth felt sorry for Bob. She could only imagine what he

thought. She shook her head. "My husband died almost three years ago. Stevie and I moved here so I could work for Mr. McDuff as nanny for his daughter. Jonathan McDuff is my employer."

"He's in love with you."

"What?"

"I said he's in love with you. Why else would he act like a jealous husband except to scare me off?"

"Oh, that's nonsense." Beth pulled on the door handle. "He hasn't spoken to me any more than necessary for the last two weeks. My guess is that he thought I should have stayed with the girls instead of leaving them for the housekeeper to watch. But he told me I should go out and do things, so that's what I'm going to do."

She opened the door and stepped out. "Are you coming?"

Bob joined her at the back of the car and together they walked into the church. He leaned close and said, "Let's not worry about it. We came to enjoy ourselves. I suggest we do that."

Beth couldn't have agreed with him more. Just thinking that Jon might be in love with her was ridiculous. So why couldn't she dislodge Bob's words from her mind?

Beth spoke to several people as they stopped to chat with her and Bob. She tried to associate names and faces since she knew very few by name beyond Larry Dauber, the Sunday school teacher, and Daniel Bozeman, their pastor.

"Don't worry." Bob seemed to sense her shyness. "In time you will learn who everyone is. Shall we go sit down?"

The fellowship hall had been decorated with a Mexican theme in keeping with the missionary emphasis of their Sunday school class.

Teenagers from the church acted as waitresses and waiters. Beth was impressed with the service and the food. Just as if they were in a restaurant, they were allowed to place an order from a menu. Beth chose a taco salad and a bean burrito.

Bob recovered well from their bad start. While they ate, he asked Beth about her life before Kansas City and listened as she talked. She noticed that he made no reference to her present job, and she assumed he would prefer to forget about Jon. He also talked about himself. She learned that he had never been married and was rapidly approaching his thirtieth birthday.

"I'd like to marry someday and have a family." He smiled at her. "Maybe in time I will. How about you? Do you think you'll ever marry again?"

"No, I don't think so." Beth forced the image of Jon from her mind. "I loved my husband very much."

Bob shook his head. "You may be surprised by what God has in store for you. You're young yet. Don't close your mind to His will."

Several minutes later, Beth thought of Bob's advice when the Sunday school teacher stood and asked for attention. "I've been asked to give a short devotional tonight. So if you brought a Bible, please turn to Judges 16:20. If you didn't bring your Bible, that's fine. Just listen along with me and let God speak from His Word to your heart."

He lifted his Bible and began to read: "But he did not know that the Lord had departed from him."

Beth listened to Larry expound on the scripture he had just read and his words pricked her heart. He said, "This day when Samson lived seems to have a special theme that we might recognize today. It is this: 'Every man did that which was right in his own eyes.' In Proverbs 14:12, it says, 'There is a way that seems right to a man, but its end is the way of death.' Doesn't that sound like Kansas City today?"

He listed several common sins and said, "People don't recognize the wrong in what they do." Then his voice dropped. "But let's get closer to home. We're all Christians here, right?

We don't do those things I mentioned. So what about the flip side? What is it we are not doing? Are we going on about our lives without seeking God's will? He has a plan for your life. Ask Him what it is and then walk ye in it."

Beth realized she had been trying to order her life the way she thought God wanted her to. She had been trying to do right. But all along God had wanted her to do His will as He saw fit for her to do. How could she know what was right for her life without direction from God? She determined to spend more time in prayer and Bible reading. She would listen to God speak through His Word and through the gentle nudge to her conscience that she had been so prone to ignore in the past.

Beth bowed her head with the others as Larry prayed. She prayed that God would take care of her future and that she would be able to step aside and allow Him to control the outcome of her employment with Jonathan. She realized now that she had been worrying about losing her girls when all along she should have been trusting God to take care of the situation.

With her trust placed in God's capable hands, Beth's heart felt lighter than it had in weeks. She smiled and spoke to those around her and Bob. As they left, she stopped long enough to tell Larry that she appreciated his devotional.

He smiled. "Thank you. I'm glad it was of help. I hope you enjoyed the banquet. The food? Was it all right?"

"Oh, yes. I love Mexican food." Beth allowed Bob to nudge her toward the door.

He kept his hand at her waist as they walked to his car. He helped her in the car, then drove the short distance to the McDuff house.

Beth saw lights on in the lower front of the house and hoped Jon had not decided to wait up for her there. Bob opened her door. As she crawled out of the car, he reached for her hand and together they walked to the front steps. On the porch, she turned to Bob.

"Thank you for taking me. I enjoyed the banquet and the devotional very much. Until tonight I hadn't realized how much I was trying to control my own life with no concern for God's will."

Bob nodded. "It's hard to let go, isn't it? I can't begin to tell you how many times I've gotten in God's way to my own detriment."

Beth looked up at Bob. He seemed to be such a nice Christian man, and he seemed to like her. If she must marry again, why not to someone like Bob? Why not Bob?

Bob leaned closer to Beth. She knew he intended to kiss her. She lifted her face toward his as the door behind her jerked open.

Stevie's screams filled the night. Beth swung to encounter Jon holding the crying baby. His shirt was unbuttoned at the neck and both sleeves had been rolled up to the elbows. Beth couldn't tear her eyes from him. Then he spoke, and Stevie's distress reached her.

"Can you do something here, Beth? I can't get her to go to sleep. I think she needs her mother."

Beth focused on Stevie, and then and took her from Jon. She cradled her against her shoulder and patted her back. The crying stopped even before she pushed past Jon into the house.

"See, I knew she just needed you." Jon started to close the door when Beth turned and saw Bob still standing on the porch, a stunned expression on his face.

"Oh, I'm sorry." She nudged Jon out of the way. "I didn't mean to just walk away, but Stevie. . . You understand, don't you?"

Bob nodded. "Yes, of course. I'll see you in the morning at church, Beth." He turned then, and Beth watched him step off the porch before Jon pulled the door closed.

twelve

The next morning, Jon stood in front of the mirror in his downstairs bathroom and shaved. When he finished, he looked into the mirror and shook his head. "You should be ashamed of the way you treated Beth last night."

When his mirror image didn't respond, he answered, "Yes, but Beth shouldn't be kissing other men on my front porch."

He turned from the mirror and went into his bedroom. His shirt and pants lay where he had tossed them on the bed. He slipped into the pants and picked up his shirt.

He wasn't ashamed of interrupting Beth's kiss even if he should be. Actually, he still thrilled at the way things had worked out. Bob What's-His-Name probably wouldn't be back. But that was okay. Beth didn't need that guy. Didn't she know that dating could lead to marriage? And the man she married would be Stevie's stepfather. The very thought soured Jon's stomach.

He slipped into his shirt and buttoned it.

No, he wasn't at all ashamed of his actions. When he'd looked out the window and saw Beth standing on his porch holding hands with Bob, his stomach had curled. Then when they started to kiss, something had snapped inside. He forgot all about Stevie when he jerked the door open with such force. He sure hoped Beth never found out that Stevie was asleep in his arms until he opened the door. Of course, he hadn't lied. Stevie wanted her mother all right. She must have. She stopped crying as soon as Beth took her.

Jon sat on the bed to put on his socks and shoes.

What bothered him more than anything was the jealousy

that raged inside him when Beth had come downstairs looking like she had just stepped out of a fashion magazine. She never dressed up like that for him when he took her anywhere. With her dark hair done up on her head, she looked sophisticated—like someone he didn't know. Maybe like someone he would like to know.

He stood and ran a comb through his hair, damp from the shower. He'd grab a tie and coat later, but right now he wanted some breakfast. Satisfied that he looked all right for church, he left his room and went around to the kitchen.

Jon hesitated at the door to the kitchen when he saw that Beth and the girls were already there. Unsure what kind of reception he would receive, he crossed the room to the refrigerator.

"Where's Mrs. Garrett?" He spoke without looking at Beth.

"She's already had breakfast and gone. She said something about meeting an old friend before church."

"Oh." Jon took a gallon jug of milk out and set it on the table next to a box of cereal. Next he kissed first Stevie, then Lexie.

"How are my girls this morning?" He avoided looking at Beth, although he could see from his peripheral vision that she watched him.

"Dada." Lexie dropped her spoon against her plate of oatmeal and toast and reached for him.

"Dada." Stevie grinned, flashing her dimple at him. She continued to eat.

Every time Lexie called him Dada, a warm glow filled his heart, but when Stevie said the word, the warm glow burned brighter than ever. Each day he thanked God for giving his daughter back to him.

He got a bowl and spoon before sitting beside Lexie. As he pulled in his chair, his foot hit something that rolled. He looked down and picked up a sippy cup.

"Is this yours, Lexie?" He grinned and handed it to her.

Temporarily satisfied, Lexie took the cup and drank her milk.

"She dropped it just before you came in," Beth said.

"I see."

"The girls got up early this morning. I thought they would be hungry."

Before Jon could respond, Stevie slapped her spoon against her tray, sending a glob of oatmeal across the table to land within inches of Jon's bowl of cereal. Lexie clapped her hands and giggled. Stevie grinned and tried to repeat the performance only this time with an empty spoon.

"Maybe we should disarm her before she figures out where the ammunition is," Jon said.

Beth reached across the corner of the table for Stevie's spoon just as Lexie decided to send her oatmeal flying. Her spoon hit the tray and, just as Stevie's had done, a glob of oatmeal became airborne. Only Lexie's missile made contact with Beth's jaw line.

Jon watched the expression on Beth's face change from shock to determination in the space of seconds. He clamped his mouth shut to keep from laughing out loud. Even then a soft snort must have escaped because, as Beth wiped the gooey oatmeal from her face, she turned toward him with a glare.

"Your daughter needs to learn some table manners."

Jon grinned at her. "Which one?"

Beth grabbed Stevie's spoon and reached for Lexie's. "Both."

Then, as if she realized what she had just said, Beth frowned. She cleared the girls' trays, leaving the toast for them to munch on and sat back down. "I guess they weren't as hungry as I thought they would be."

Jon tackled his cereal, keeping quiet until he finished.

When the girls began shredding their toast and dropping

pieces on the floor, Jon and Beth reacted at the same time. Jon scooped Lexie up and Beth took Stevie.

Jon couldn't keep from laughing at the happy expression on his little girl's face. Lexie had been a quiet child until Stevie came. Now she splashed her bath water and threw her food. He'd even seen her and Stevie in a tussle over a toy the other day.

Jon glanced at Beth as she cleaned Stevie's face and hands. Yes, bringing Stevie into his house had been good for Lexie. But what about him? Had bringing Beth into his home complicated his life more than he could handle? What if he fell in love with her? What if he already had? Was that why he'd been so jealous of Bob What's-His-Name?

An hour later, Jon took Lexie to church, dropping her off at the nursery as usual. He sat beside his parents and tried to listen to the sermon, but the image of Beth kept getting in his way. Beth, in jeans and T-shirt, her dark hair held back out of the way in a ponytail, playing with the girls. Beth, beautiful in a soft blue dress, getting ready to go out with another man. His thoughts skidded to a stop as red-hot jealousy again surged through his heart.

He shifted in the seat. How long did Pastor Barnes intend to preach this morning, anyway? Thoughts of Beth at that very moment sitting in church with Bob kept Jon occupied and restless throughout the rest of the service.

As soon as church ended, Jon spoke to his parents, then headed for the nursery to pick up Lexie. By the time he pulled into his own driveway, his nerves were on edge. He and Lexie went in search of Beth and found her in the kitchen chatting with Mrs. Garrett.

She had changed into jeans and had her long hair pulled back into a ponytail. She looked like a teenager, sitting on the high stool peeling potatoes.

She dropped her knife when he walked through the door

and smiled, her eyes brightening. She reached toward him. "Hey, how's my girl? Did you miss me as much as I missed you?"

Lexie wiggled in his arms, trying to get to her mother. Jon blinked as he realized Beth's smile was not meant for him. Feeling foolish, he stepped closer and Lexie fell into Beth's arms. Beth cuddled the baby, talking to her, totally ignoring him.

Stevie toddled toward him from somewhere in the room. He hadn't even thought to ask where she was. She lifted her arms and he picked her up, glad that someone wanted him.

"I'm going outside with Stevie. Do you want me to take Lexie, too?"

Beth's eyes met his as if she'd just realized he was there. "Oh, I guess I should get these potatoes peeled. Mary is always helping with the girls, so I thought I'd give her a hand. Besides, I love to cook."

As Jon took Lexie from Beth, he said, "My parents are coming over this afternoon. They want to see the girls."

"How nice. It will be good to see them again."

Jon sat on the patio in the fenced-in backyard and watched the girls explore. He really should have changed his clothes, but he'd been in a hurry to get away from Beth. Why that was, he didn't know. He'd wanted to come home badly enough during church.

Frustrated at himself for acting like a love-struck teenager, he shoved all thoughts of Beth aside and concentrated on the little girls. He did pretty well, too, until Lexie brought a yellow dandelion to him and looked up at him with Beth's large, blue eyes.

❧

By Monday morning, Jon couldn't wait to get to his office as an escape from Beth's sweet temptation. He swiveled away from his desk and looked out the window at the busy city below and wondered, for not the first time, if he had done the right thing in bringing Beth and Stevie into his home. At the time, his only thoughts had been for his daughter—to bring her home where she belonged. He hadn't considered that her mother might turn out to be so appealing. But beautiful as she might be on the outside, Beth's goal was to ultimately win both girls from him.

And that he would not allow. Maybe he should ask Beth to leave. He could set her up in an apartment nearby so he could visit Stevie. He shoved his chair back and stood, then paced from one side of his office to the other. What if he did such a thing? Would she stay there, or would she take Stevie and move back to Bolivar? She might even decide to fight him for Lexie. Maybe things would be better left alone.

Frustrated with his life and his pacing, Jon left his office and went in search of his father.

Ray McDuff looked up, the telephone against his ear. As Jon sank into the chair in front of his desk, he brought his conversation to a close and hung up the receiver.

"Well, you look more like a thundercloud than those outside. What can I do for you, Son?"

Jon glanced toward the window. He had been looking outside for over an hour and hadn't noticed the rain. If that wasn't a sure sign of the turmoil Beth had caused in his life, he didn't know what was.

"I have no idea. I haven't been able to think since Stevie and her mother showed up."

Ray burst out laughing.

"I'm serious, Dad." Jon stood and moved around the room. "Stevie's mother has me tied up in knots." He swung toward his father. "Or is she Lexie's mother? All I know is that she's caused more turmoil in my house in the month or so that she's been there than Sharolyn caused in three years."

"Hmm." Ray leaned back in his chair and made a steeple

with his fingers, resting his hands across his stomach. "Judging from my memories of Sharolyn, that would have to be a considerable amount of turmoil. Just what is it this woman does?"

Jon opened his mouth to speak and promptly shut it. How could he tell his father that Beth was seeing another man and just thinking about it drove him up the wall? He tried another angle. "She wants both the girls. I think the best thing would be for her to move out into an apartment."

"I see." Ray nodded. "And you think she would be willing to do that, considering she wants both girls?"

"No." Jon paced to the other side of the room and straightened a picture on the wall. "She isn't going anywhere. She can't because of the babies. How could she leave Lexie now? Or Stevie? And I'd never let her take either of them. Not now."

He dropped back into the chair in front of his father. "Can't you see my problem? Those two little girls tie Beth and me together tighter than most marriage vows. So how do I get out of it? How do I get my life back to normal?"

"What about Beth? Do you have any complaints with her mothering skills?"

Jon shook his head. "No. She's perfect. I mean as a mother. She treats the girls equally. She's always with them, but she doesn't crowd them. She makes sure they are clean and fed. She sleeps with her door cracked open so she can hear them at night. She takes them outside every day and plays with them. No one could find fault with Beth's treatment of the girls."

Ray's voice softened. "You know she has as much right to those babies as you do, don't you?"

Jon nodded.

Ray chuckled then, and Jon looked up as he said, "I just had a thought. If you want to make sure you don't lose Stevie again, why don't you and Beth adopt each other's biological child? Then we could draw up a contract for equal custody.

You could kick Beth out of your house and still retain visiting rights. Ingenious plan, don't you think?"

"Ha-ha." Jon stood and moved toward the door. "I'm sure there must be some humor in there somewhere, Dad. Sorry I don't see it."

He went back to his own office with his father's laughter ringing in his ears.

ತಿ

Beth loved early spring when flowers began to bloom and green spread across the land. She took the girls outside after their afternoon nap and watched them run through the grass and play. The rain clouds of that morning had all but disappeared in the face of sunshine and a gentle breeze.

"Hi. Mary said I'd find you out here."

Beth looked up from Stevie's investigation of a colony of ants that were rebuilding their hill after the rain. She smiled at Cecelia and watched Robbie run after Lexie. "Hi. What are you two doing out on a Monday afternoon? I thought lawyers worked long, hard hours winning all those cases in court."

Cecelia laughed. "That's the advantage of working for one's father. I used to work long, hard hours, but since Robbie was born, I've cut back. Now I only accept the easy cases and I take off work whenever the urge to shop hits. How about it? Want to go with us?"

Beth stood and dusted her hands together. "Wow! I'm impressed with your persuasive techniques. No wonder you don't have to work twelve-hour days. You've already talked me into a shopping trip."

Cecelia laughed again. "All right! Let's get these munchkins gathered up, outfitted, and in my van. My credit card is burning a hole in my wallet as we stand here talking."

Beth laughed and grabbed Stevie as she started away. "Come on, let's get your sister and go bye-bye."

Cecelia drove to the nearest mall and parked.

As they pulled babies and strollers from the van, Beth shook her head. "You must have been desperate for company to ask us to come along. Look at all this."

Cecelia laughed. "I thrive on babies and shopping. It's such a welcome relief from my high-pressure job. And I'll enjoy getting better acquainted with my two nieces not to mention their mother."

Beth cast a side glance toward Cecelia as she pushed her girls in a bulky twin stroller and Cecelia guided a small umbrella stroller holding her son toward the mall entrance. "Do you feel at all uncomfortable about our situation? I mean, having Stevie and me show up this way. It must have been a shock."

"Oh, yeah." Cecelia nodded. "But a pleasant shock. Look what we got out of it. Two absolutely adorable little girls. Surely you can understand when I say that Stevie and Lexie are equally my nieces. I couldn't choose between them if I had to and I bet you couldn't either."

"No, I couldn't."

Cecelia gave Beth a wide smile, then headed toward the children's clothing store. Three hours later, the back of the van piled with packages, the women headed home with three sleepy children. Cecelia turned down the street toward Jon's house. "That was fun. Next time let's go to the park."

"Sure." Beth smiled. She liked Cecelia.

"Good. That's settled, so now we'll work on the dude ranch."

Beth straightened from the headrest and turned to face Cecelia. "Dude ranch? You are going to work on a dude ranch?"

Cecelia laughed. "Each year, my brothers and I, along with our spouses, go to a dude ranch out in Kansas for a weekend trip. It's just a fun thing we've done for years. I want you to come with Jon."

Beth gasped as she understood Cecelia's meaning. "Wait just a minute. I, by no stretch of the imagination, am Jon's spouse."

"Of course you aren't. Donna went before she and Brad were married. You can, too."

Beth shook her head. "No, I don't think so."

"Oh, come on. It'll be fun. You don't want to leave me stuck with Donna for female companionship, do you? I mean Donna is all right, but she's. . .well, she's Donna."

Beth smiled. Then she sobered. "I'm sorry, but Jon would never want me to go. If he asked, maybe, but don't hold your breath because he won't."

"You like him, don't you?"

"Jon? Sure, I like him fine."

"Come on, Beth. Don't play games. You know what I'm asking. There's something going on between you two. He's different even at work. And there are sparks when you are together. I admit I haven't been around you a lot, but it doesn't take long to see that you two were made for each other."

"I don't think so." Beth shook her head. "Even if I felt something for him, we both have our past marriages to consider. I loved Steven very much. I'm sure Jon still has feelings for his wife."

"Oh, I'm sure he does." Cecelia stopped in the driveway and turned off the motor. She turned to face Beth. "Let's see if I can tell you about Sharolyn before the kids start a ruckus. She was not your typical wife. I have no idea why Jon married her. She wanted his money. Period."

Beth's eyes widened and Cecelia nodded. "I'm serious. But that's not the worst. What she didn't want was a baby. When she got pregnant, she tried to get an abortion, but Jon threatened to kick her out and tie the purse strings if she harmed Stevie in the slightest."

Cecelia looked away from Beth as she continued. "They

had a fight the night she died. She threatened to end the baby's life, then she was in that car accident."

She turned back to Beth. "You know about the pileup that caused the babies to be switched?"

At Beth's nod, Cecelia said, "Sharolyn veered across the oncoming lanes of traffic. She caused the wreck that took her life. Jon thinks she was trying to kill the baby. I think she was taking something that made her crazy. Not that she needed much help." That last Cecelia said under her breath.

When Beth didn't say anything, she went on, "I've seen Jon look at you. I know he cares for you more than he will admit to right now. Give him time. He needs to sort out the facts and discover that he can trust another woman. Right now, he doesn't trust anyone. Sharolyn tried to kill his child. He thinks you are trying to take both of his babies away from him."

As Beth started to protest, Cecelia held up her hand. "I know. You've seen how much he loves them. But can you honestly say that the thought of running away with both of your babies has never crossed your mind?"

Beth could only stare at the other woman.

As Stevie started to fuss, Cecelia said, "You know, I think you are more attracted to Jon than you want to admit even to yourself. Think about what I've said. See if you can't understand him a little better. Then give him a chance and come with us to the dude ranch."

Beth nodded. "I'll promise to think about things. But that's all I can do. I won't go where I'm not wanted, and I'm sure Jon doesn't want me."

"Then you'll go if he invites you?"

"Yes, I'll go if he asks me."

thirteen

"How about it, Beth? Will you go with us?"

Beth looked across the table at Jon and laughed. "As if you'd take both these babies to a petting zoo by yourself."

His dimple flashed and his eyes twinkled. "Is that a yes?"

At that moment, Beth realized she had a weakness for people with just one dimple—first Stevie and now Jon. She gave in gracefully. "Yes, I'll go with you. I wouldn't want the girls eaten by a lion."

Jon's eyebrows lifted. "You do know petting zoos don't have lions, don't you?"

"Of course." Beth helped Stevie scoop corn with her spoon. "But if I don't go along, you might go to the wrong zoo."

Jon laughed and caught Lexie's spoon just before she dropped it over the side of her highchair tray. "Mrs. Garrett, how about you coming, too? It sounds like I need all the help I can get."

Mary shook her head and smiled. "No thanks. By the time these two babies finish their lunch, I'll have plenty to do."

"I'm sorry, Mary. Stevie has been a bad influence on Lexie, hasn't she?" Beth handed the spoon to Stevie after an unsuccessful attempt to feed her. Stevie and Lexie both were becoming more independent with each day.

"Not a bad influence, Beth." Mary stood and picked up her plate, then she stacked Jon's and Beth's plates on top of hers. "I'd say it's been good for her. Lexie has come alive since she has a sister to play with. She was too good before."

"Too good?" Beth smiled. "I can't imagine saying that about Stevie. She always had day-care kids to play with from the time

124

I brought her home. I suppose she learned a lot from them."

"Maybe some of that feistiness is inherited." Mary slanted a glance toward Jon, who had his hands full trying to get Lexie to either use her spoon or leave it on the tray.

After several near misses, he caught the spoon and put in on the table out of her reach. An ear-piercing yowl announced her displeasure as she arched back against the seat with both hands pushing against the tray.

Mary laughed. "And then again, maybe not."

Beth pushed her chair back to take care of Lexie, but Jon had her in his arms before she could get there. He carried her out of the kitchen. Beth could hear him talking to her as he went.

"Now, is that any way to act at the table? Let's calm down and get cleaned up so we can go bye-bye."

Beth didn't know if Lexie calmed down or if Jon had walked out of hearing range, but she couldn't hear any more screams. While Mary continued clearing the table, Beth helped Stevie finish her lunch, then took her from her high-chair. As she went upstairs, she realized she hadn't once thought that Jon might hurt Lexie. She had completely trusted him to handle her baby without fear that he would harm her in any way. At that moment, she realized that she trusted Jon not only with the babies, but with her very life, even with her heart.

Beth found Jon and Lexie in the bathroom. He looked up from the tub of water where Lexie sat playing with a rubber alligator mother and her three babies.

"She had mashed potatoes in her hair. I figured a bath wouldn't hurt."

Beth smiled. "I see. It not only gets her clean, but playing in the water does wonders for helping her forget her little temper tantrum."

Jon grinned and shrugged. "Sure. You want to put Stevie in here, too?"

"As soon as you get Lexie out. I've found that I get a whole lot less wet when I do one at a time."

"Good thinking." Jon picked up a towel and held it out toward Lexie. "Come on, sweetheart. Let's go bye-bye."

As Jon took Lexie from the water, Beth moved deeper into the bathroom and got Stevie ready for her bath. Just as Jon stepped out into the hall, she stopped him. "I bought some new outfits for the girls the other day. They are hanging in the closet."

"How am I supposed to recognize them?"

"Easy. They still have the tags on."

"Okay. Which one is Lexie's?"

Beth shrugged. "It doesn't matter. They are just alike." She called after him as he moved away, "And the same size."

By the time Beth and Stevie got to the nursery, Jon had Lexie almost dressed. He spoke without taking his attention from the tiny buttons on the back of the white dress with red and blue stars of various sizes on it. "These are cute. Kind of patriotic."

"That's the idea. Red, white, and blue for the Fourth of July. It's close enough that I thought they could break them in today."

Beth pulled Stevie's matching dress and diaper cover from the closet and soon had her dressed. She looked at the two babies. Except for their eye color and facial features, the girls looked remarkably alike in their new outfits. No wonder they had been switched without anyone suspecting. If their blood type hadn't been so different, the error might never have been discovered.

"Are you ready to go?" Jon held Lexie. "Where's the double stroller?"

"In the hall closet downstairs. I used it when we went shopping with Cecelia."

Beth went through the door ahead of Jon and thought

how domestic so much of their conversation sounded. She took Lexie while he got the stroller and opened the outside door for her. Then together they walked to his van, and Beth waited with the girls while he unlocked the doors. While he stowed the stroller in the back, she slipped Stevie into her car seat. By then Jon took over and fastened Stevie into the seat while Beth went to the other side and secured Lexie into her seat.

All of this was done as a matter of course. *Just like a married couple*, Beth thought before she realized where her thoughts were headed. She got in front next to Jon and glanced at him as she buckled her seatbelt. Nothing had changed in their relationship. Why would she think of Jon as anything other than Stevie's biological father? To make sure it didn't happen again, she concentrated on the houses and buildings outside her window as they passed.

At the zoo, Jon took Stevie while Beth got Lexie, and together they buckled them into the double stroller. Beth noticed several people stop to smile at the babies. They obviously thought the girls were twins. Beth knew that she would have a hard time convincing a stranger that they were actually no blood relation at all. And for a reason she didn't take time to analyze, she didn't care. Instead, she enjoyed the second looks that almost everyone gave them.

What did bother Beth was when she found herself daydreaming that she and Jon and the girls were a family on a Sunday afternoon outing.

"Let's go see the lambs first." Jon pushed the stroller while Beth walked beside him.

The petting zoo, located next to the main zoo, was not large. With only three or four fenced-off yards, Beth figured it wouldn't take long to pet every animal in the zoo. What she didn't count on was the girl's enthusiasm for the animals.

Jon took Stevie from the stroller and knelt beside a fluffy

white lamb. "Mine housh." Stevie grabbed an armful of lamb and held on.

"Housh?" Jon looked up at Beth. "What does that mean?"

Beth giggled. "I think it means she intends to take it home with her."

Lexie wanted the same lamb. Beth set her down and knelt beside her.

With both hands reaching, Lexie squatted beside the baby lamb. Before Beth or Jon realized what she had in mind, she slapped the little animal on its side with her open hands. The lamb jerked and squirmed free from Stevie, letting out a sound guaranteed to bring his mother if she had been nearby. Stevie's face crumpled and she wailed. Lexie looked from the lamb, now on his feet running away, to Stevie, and she began to cry.

With both babies crying at the top of their lungs, Jon and Beth became the center of attention. Beth stood with Lexie clutched close and wished she could disappear.

"Now what?" Jon looked like he shared her thought as he tried to quiet Stevie.

"I think we make a rapid exit before we're thrown out." Beth reached for the stroller and Jon's hand closed over hers.

Jon jerked his hand away. "I'm sorry."

Was he apologizing for touching her? Beth carried Lexie and pushed the stroller away from the enclosed area to the center of the zoo. By that time, the girls' tears had subsided, so they buckled them into the stroller.

"Do we risk another encounter or go home while we are ahead?"

By encounter, Beth didn't know whether Jon meant holding hands or petting animals. Her hand still tingled where he had touched it. She decided to play it safe and assume he meant the animals. She grimaced. "This was your idea. You decide."

Jon looked around the zoo and shrugged. "I'm willing to try

again if you are. Should we go with a larger animal or a smaller one?"

"Maybe a larger one could defend itself better."

Jon indicated the pen holding a few goats, calves, one large camel, and several other similar animals. A sign advertised a pony ride for three dollars. Several children and their parents moved from one animal to another. "Maybe one of those?"

Beth nodded. "That might be safe enough if we wait a few years on the pony ride."

Jon grinned. "I agree. I don't know what we would do if our daughters started a stampede."

"Can a person die of embarrassment?" Beth's question brought a chuckle from Jon.

"I think they just wish they could."

When Beth reached the gate, Jon leaned around her to open it. She felt his hand touch her waist as if to guide her as she pushed the stroller into the pen and wondered if he realized what he was doing.

After the episode with the baby lamb, Jon and Beth kept a closer watch on the girls. Stevie and Lexie took turns sitting on a calf and touching one of the goats. They were both afraid of the camel when it turned to look at them. After that, Jon decided they could pet the smaller animals. So they held rabbits, kittens, and puppies. Then Beth held a down-covered duck in her hand and let the girls take turns touching it with Jon's supervision.

By the time Jon said they had seen enough animals for one day, both girls were ready for a nap and fell asleep before they left the parking lot.

On the way home, Jon glanced toward Beth. He finally spoke when he stopped at a stoplight. "Do you ride?"

Thinking of the animals they had just seen, Beth assumed he didn't mean in an automobile. "If you mean horses, the answer is probably no."

"Yes, I meant horses. My family goes to a dude ranch in Kansas every year in June. I thought you might like to go with us. You don't have to know how to ride. Just be willing to sit in the saddle and let the horse walk. They have some pretty tame horses."

"What about the girls?"

Jon grinned at her. "Our parents don't go. They want the girls for the weekend. And Robbie." He laughed. "They don't have any idea what they are getting into."

Beth smiled. "That's true, but—"

"It also gives Mrs. Garrett a chance to get away for the weekend. She always looks forward to us being gone." Had Jon interrupted to keep her from turning him down?

"Did Cecelia tell you to ask me?" Beth knew the answer before she asked.

The light changed and Jon drove through the intersection. He shrugged. "She suggested that I ask, but I really want you to go." He turned just enough so she could see his dimple when he grinned. "Please."

Disappointment dampened Beth's eagerness to spend an entire weekend with Jon. Knowing that the invitation had not originated with him warned her that she would not actually be with him, but she found that her desire for whatever crumbs he handed her overrode what little common sense she had left in his presence.

Beth's lips twitched as a smile formed. "All right. I'll go, but someone will have to help me stay on the horse if I go riding."

"Oh, you'll go riding. We always go on a trail ride on Saturday morning." Again his dimple flashed her way. "Don't worry. I'll see that you stay in the saddle."

❧

Cecelia called Thursday morning. "Hey, are you ready to go shopping again?"

Beth laughed. "Shopping? I thought we'd be going to the park."

"We can do that, too. After we shop." Cecelia's voice bubbled over the line. "I've already talked to Mom. She's agreed to watch our little darlings while we find some great cowgirl clothes. Come on, we'll have fun. And just think—no strollers."

"All right." Beth gave in. "If you promise we can pick the kids up afterward and take them to the park."

Cecelia laughed. "You are a glutton for punishment, Beth."

"Only when it comes to my two girls," Beth said.

"Jon's a lucky man this time around."

Beth wondered if she had heard right. "I think you lost me on that one."

Cecelia's laughter came over the line. "Don't worry. I'll explain myself later if you haven't figured it out by then."

Beth changed into slacks and a short-sleeved top. She pulled her checkbook out and looked at the balance. Jon's generosity and the fact that she seldom found anything to spend money on had brought her account to an all-time high. Working as a nanny had its advantages. Of course, falling in love with the boss wasn't one of them.

Stevie had grown to love her ma-maw and pa-paw over the past few months. They doted on her and Lexie both. Beth watched Jon's mother gather the girls and Robbie into her arms as if she hadn't seen them in years instead of days. She knew they would be fine, yet she felt a stab of disappointment that neither girl seemed to mind when she and Cecelia left.

An experienced shopper, Cecelia took Beth to the best stores. Before the morning was over, she had purchased several new outfits including a pair of designer jeans and one red plaid, snap-front Western shirt. Beth questioned the necessity of the shirt for just one weekend, especially when she considered the cost of her purchases.

"But it won't be just one weekend," Cecelia explained. "I told you we go every year and, besides, you can wear it anytime you want to. You look great in red with your dark coloring."

Beth still wasn't convinced. "You go every year. That doesn't mean I will."

Cecelia smiled. "Oh, yes, it does. A wife always goes with her husband."

She laughed at Beth's shocked expression. "Oh, come on. You may as well face it. Jon is in love with you. Just as much as you are with him."

Beth shook her head even as her heart pounded with hope. "I think you are seeing things. Jon is not in love with me."

"He invited you to go to the ranch, didn't he?"

"Yes, but that doesn't mean he loves me. He only invited me because you wanted him to."

"Did he say that?"

"No, but—"

"I know what I see. Jon has changed so much since you and Stevie arrived on the scene. I've not seen him so alive since his pre-Sharolyn days. Jon loves you. Just give him time to figure it out for himself."

Beth didn't argue further. Time would tell, then Cecelia would realize she had been wrong.

fourteen

Beth surveyed the room she had been assigned at the Triple T Dude Ranch. In the center of the room, a braided rug, made from wool strips of various autumn colors, covered the wood floor. The double bed, covered with a Lone Star quilt that repeated the warm tones of orange, yellow, and brown, hugged one wall. The dresser against the opposite wall looked as if it had been there for generations. Its chipped mirror returned a wavy image, although Beth could see anticipation and fear in her own eyes well enough.

Along with the antique furnishings, the lack of either telephone or TV gave the appearance of a time gone by. Beth smiled. She had never been on a ranch before, but she liked her room. It certainly beat the image she'd had of them sleeping out in the bunk house next to the horses.

"Hey, are you ready for supper?" Cecelia stuck her head in Beth's doorway.

"Supper?"

Cecelia giggled. "Yes, that's what we call dinner when we play cowboy. Here we eat breakfast, dinner, and supper, in that order."

"Let's go, then."

"Do you like your room?" Cecelia gave Beth just enough time to nod before she began a steady stream of chatter that lasted all the way downstairs and into the large dining room.

The others were all there, including two couples Beth had not seen before. As the guests moved toward the long oak table, Cecelia joined her husband, Rob, leaving Beth alone.

"Hi." Jon reached past Beth to pull out a chair. He motioned for her to sit. When she did, he took the space next to her.

After they ate, everyone gathered on the wide front porch overlooking the long drive to the road. Beth could see a line of trees in the distance and a few shade trees stood in the yard, but most of the land surrounding the house stood open. Running as far as she could see in either direction from the drive were white wooden fences that formed holding pens for the horses near the barn and other outbuildings.

All evening, Beth had been aware that the guests were paired off. All but she and Jon. Was that why Jon sat with her at supper? If so, why had he moved so far away now? She looked across the porch where Jon sat leaning against a post, one knee drawn up with his arm resting on it. She wished she had enough nerve to join him. But she knew if he'd wanted to be with her, he would have stayed by her side after supper.

The rest of the guests sat in chairs or on the floor of the porch by twos. Gene and Carol Altman, the ranch owners, occupied the porch swing. Some couples held hands, others cuddled, but all touched. A breeze ruffled Beth's hair before moving on. She sat on the porch railing and leaned against a corner post. Over a dozen people filled the Altmans' front porch, and she felt more alone than she had in a long time.

A couple of ranch hands strummed guitars while they sang some songs that Beth imagined had been heard long ago on the range while cowboys camped on the long cattle drives. When they sang "Home on the Range" and "Get Along Little Doggie," everyone joined in.

They sang several songs while the sun sank below the western horizon, throwing out rays of orange and red against the wispy clouds overhead. Beth watched the spectacular sunset for several minutes before looking across the porch at Jon. He didn't smile but held her gaze. She felt as if they were together in the night as the music faded into background noise, and her vision narrowed to include only Jon. How she would love to know what his thoughts and feelings were at that moment.

"Well?" Cecelia's voice beside her brought Beth back to reality.

She looked at Jon's sister and realized that the smug expression on her face meant she had witnessed Beth's preoccupation with her brother.

"The rest of us are heading to bed." Cecelia held her husband's arm as he talked to another man. "You probably didn't hear Carol say that morning on a ranch comes early."

No, Beth hadn't heard. She hoped the darkness hid the flush that covered her face. "Why is that? Why do we get up early, I mean?"

"The trail ride starts about midmorning. Before that, we have to check the horses and do some ranch-type work. Don't worry, it's fun to pretend you're a real ranch hand." Cecelia cupped her hand around her mouth to whisper to Beth. "Actually, we don't have to get up all that early. Just because we are from the city, they think we sleep till noon every day." As Robert turned his attention to his wife, she said, "The country air makes it easy to get to sleep, though, so I'm heading upstairs."

Beth watched Cecelia and Robert go inside, then turned to look for Jon but found the porch almost deserted as everyone heeded Mrs. Altman's promise of an early morning. Jon had gone without waiting to walk with her. A stab of disappointment pricked her heart, and she followed the other guests inside.

As Cecelia predicted, Beth had no trouble getting to sleep. When she awoke at six the next morning, she listened for the usual sounds of two little girls playing in their cribs and heard nothing. Then the call of a bird outside her window caught her attention. Somewhere below, probably at the barn, a man yelled something she couldn't understand. The house remained quiet, so Beth assumed the hired hands got up even earlier than the guests.

She threw back the light sheet she had used for a cover and sat up. If she hurried, she could get in and out of the shower before anyone else awoke.

As Beth came out of the shower, she heard what sounded like a dinner bell clanging. She had started to wear her new expensive jeans and western shirt, but after Cecelia's promise that she would be working like a ranch hand, she opted for the old pair of jeans and shirt she'd packed. Cecelia might not mind getting muck and dirt on her designer jeans, but Beth did.

She could hear people stirring from one end of the second floor to the other. Doors opened and closed, and the murmur of voices drifted through her open door. Beth sat on her bed and pulled on the new boots Cecelia had insisted were necessary equipment for life on a ranch.

With some free time on her hands while everyone else dressed, Beth reached for her Bible and read from the Psalms. Then, as others began drifting downstairs, she grabbed her hat and, feeling like a real cowgirl, clomped down the stairs to the dining room.

The aroma of bacon and eggs caused her stomach to growl as she sat in the chair Jon held for her. She glanced at him as he sat beside her and wondered if the only time she'd be near him was when they ate.

He flashed a grin her way. "Hi, how did you sleep?"

"Fine."

"What's wrong? Are you missing the girls?"

"I suppose a little. Why? Am I acting homesick?"

He chuckled. "I hope not after just one day. You just seem quieter than usual."

They bowed their heads as Gene Altman led the prayer of thanksgiving for their food. At his "Amen," Jon leaned closer to Beth. "After breakfast we'll go out to the barn. There are a few little chores we do before the ride. Carol's in charge of the kitchen, and she'll need help getting enough lunch packed for the trail ride. I know you like to cook. Would you like to help her in here while we take care of the horses?"

Would she! Beth thought of her new clothes folded out of sight in her suitcase upstairs and wished she could run up and put them on. Fixing lunch for sixteen would be easy and leave little chance of getting dirty. She smiled at Jon. "I'd love to, but how do I go about getting the job?"

"No problem." Jon leaned forward and looked toward the end of the table where Carol sat. He nodded and smiled. Carol Altman, a petite woman in her early thirties, seemed to have a perpetual smile on her face. Now her smile widened as she met Beth's curious gaze. She gave Jon a thumbs-up gesture, which he returned, and the deal was made.

"You had that prearranged," Beth accused Jon. She laughed at his innocent look. "What's wrong? Do you think I'm too much of a sissy to muck out a barn?"

Jon shrugged. "If you insist, we can always tell Carol that you've changed your mind."

"No you don't." Beth grabbed his arm as if to hold him down. "I know a good thing when I see it."

Jon didn't speak, but his eyes grew even darker as they searched her face. Beth felt as if she were tied to him in some unexplainable way. Then she became aware of her hand still on his arm and pulled it away, breaking contact. Her fingers tingled and her breath came in short bursts.

How could this be? She was not supposed to fall in love again. At the moment, she could barely remember what Steven looked like because Jon's image had replaced his. Beth cleaned her plate of pancakes with bacon and eggs simply because she felt the need to keep busy and ignore the intense attraction for the man by her side.

Jon acted as if nothing had happened, although he spoke little to her and went out of the way to avoid touching her hand when she passed the butter to him. She knew he felt the same attraction she had and was just as confused by it.

Beth breathed a sigh of relief when Jon left with the others and Carol spoke to her. "I'm so glad you offered to stay and help me. Most of our guests want to get out on the range as soon as possible and forget there are indoor chores to do as well."

"I'm glad to help."

"You're Beth, aren't you?" Carol began stacking plates, so Beth gathered the table service. "Jon mentioned that this is your first experience with a dude ranch. It's been tame so far, but we'll get out on the trail here in a little bit. Have you ridden before?"

Beth enjoyed Carol's chatter as it took her mind from Jon and the new, strange feelings she had for him. By ten o'clock, she and Carol had the dining room and kitchen clean. They had enough sandwiches, potato salad, and beans packed for sixteen people with hearty appetites. Carol insisted that by the time they stopped at noon, Beth would be able to eat twice what she normally did.

Beth patted her full stomach. "After that breakfast, I don't know how. I'll take your word for it, though. You are coming on the ride, aren't you?"

Carol nodded. "Oh, yes, I wouldn't miss it. Anymore, I don't get out as much as I'd like, so this is my way of finding time to ride."

Beth didn't know what to expect as she and Carol joined the others at the barn. Everyone appeared clean enough, although one man had a streak of mud down one leg. Beth could only imagine what had happened to him.

Jon greeted her with a smile. "You missed some fun."

"Oh, really?" Beth couldn't control the flutter deep inside that his dimple caused.

"Yeah. Johnson, the guy over there with dirt caked on his pants, thought he'd be smart and mess with Gene's stallion. Gene told him to stay away from him, that he wasn't broke yet."

"And he didn't listen." Beth shook her head. A grown man acting like a child deserved some humiliation. She was glad he hadn't been seriously hurt, though.

"Nope." Jon took Beth's arm and led her to the corral where their mounts waited. "The stallion took a side step and twist, and Johnson hit the ground in a slide—right through a mud puddle."

Beth saw the stallion Jon was talking about standing in an adjoining corral. He stood alone watching the people with wary eyes. But Beth wasn't interested in a horse she wouldn't ride. She could count the times she had ridden horseback on one hand, so her concern was for the horse that she would be riding.

"I got you a gentle one named Lady. Gene says she's been trained for beginning riders." Jon helped Beth pick her horse out of the others and stood to one side, holding the reins while she mounted.

"Lady." Beth leaned forward just enough to pat the horse's neck. "I hope you are as nice as your name."

Lady twitched her ears as if she understood. Jon rode into place beside her on a sleek brown and white horse that stood even taller than Lady. He grinned at Beth. "Are you ready to ride?"

She nodded, and the movement made her feel as if she could fall from the horse. Knowing that her fear came from a lack of confidence in her own abilities, she tightened her knees just a bit and straightened her back.

Then she sent a wide smile to Jon. "Anytime you are."

Rather than going in one long line with the horses riding nose to tail, each ranch hand took a few riders as they were ready and headed out. They would all meet at a prearranged spot for lunch. Jon and Beth went with the second group, which included Robert and Cecelia as well as the ranch hand they called Buck.

Jon and Beth rode together behind the other three. Beth wondered if Jon stayed close so he could catch her if she fell off her mount. For the first mile or so, she saw the wisdom in such a precaution before she became more comfortable in the saddle. As she relaxed, she allowed her body to move with the rhythm of the horse, and she enjoyed the ride much more than she thought she would. By the time they reached the designated stop, she felt like a seasoned cowgirl.

Jon swung off his horse as if he rode every day. Beth watched him and tried to figure out how he had gotten down so easily. While she thought about it, he appeared by her side and, with a little coaching and some hands-on help, had her on the ground.

"You may need to move around a little to loosen up your muscles."

Beth gave Jon a frown as she felt her leg and back muscles protest. "Now you tell me."

He laughed. "Don't feel bad. I'll probably be sore for a week after we get home."

"That's not much consolation." Beth made a face. "If you're going to be sore for a week, I'll be sore for two."

She noticed that Cecelia and Robert were also strolling back and forth as were several others. Why had she let Cecelia talk her into this?

The first group waited for them and the third rode over the rise within a minute or so. With the third group came the Altmans and the food. As Carol and Gene lifted the bags containing lunch from their horses, a cheer went up.

Beth found a grassy spot to eat, and Jon settled beside her. After they ate, he pulled her from the ground and helped her climb back on her horse for the return trip. From the time she saw the barn rise to full height on the distant horizon until she fell from the saddle in the barnyard, Beth longed for a soaking bath.

Thirty minutes later, after unsaddling and brushing her horse, Beth's wish was granted. Just before she closed and locked the bathroom door, Cecelia slipped her a bottle of liniment with the promise that it would help. Beth thanked her, then sank into the waiting tub of soapy water.

Three hours and a nap later, Beth woke to the clanging of the supper bell. She took one look at her new clothing still folded in her suitcase and decided this would be the perfect time to wear them.

Jon strode down the hall as Beth emerged from her room. She thought she saw a flash of appreciation in his eyes before his smile warmed her heart. He took her arm as if she belonged to him and she didn't pull away.

"Come on, pretty lady. If we don't hurry, we'll miss supper and if we miss supper, we'll miss the ride."

"Ride?" Beth's voice rose. "As in horseback riding? Again?"

Jon laughed. "Yeah, horses pulling a wagon filled with hay. I think the kids usually call it a hayride. And, yes, you are going." He paused before adding, "With me."

Beth looked up into his eyes and her heart beat against her ribs. She would go anywhere with him. Hadn't she proved that by going on this trip?

When she didn't answer but kept looking at him, his dimple deepened and he slipped his arm around her waist, stopping her just outside the dining room. "You'd better stop looking at me that way, Beth, or I won't be responsible for my actions."

❧

Less than an hour later, Beth snuggled into the hay-filled wagon close to Jon. Cecelia, sitting across from them with her husband holding her close, smiled when Jon's arm went around Beth. Beth glanced toward the red sun, slowly sinking behind the barn, and wondered if his actions were a product of the romance of the ranch.

Regardless of Jon's true motivation, Beth decided to take advantage of his nearness. She snuggled into the circle of his arm and released a soft sigh of pleasure.

"Are you glad you came?" Jon's breath caressed her ear.

She nodded, not trusting her voice to remain steady.

"Me, too." Jon pulled her against his side and repeated, "Yeah, me, too."

As the sun sank from sight and darkness covered the prairie, Beth began to believe she belonged under Jon's arm, close to his side. If only this ride could go on forever.

Much too soon, the dark silhouette of the ranch house and barn stood against the darkening sky, and Gene turned the wagon onto the long drive that led to the house.

"I guess this is it." Jon sounded as reluctant to end their moments together as she did.

Beth turned to look up at him and saw that his attention centered on her. Or, more precisely, on her lips. As his head moved, she lifted her lips to meet his. The kiss was long and sweet—and over too soon.

fifteen

Beth cuddled her two babies close. She sat on the floor in the family room in Jon's house, glad to be home. "I didn't know how much I would miss you two little sweethearts."

From the enthusiastic greeting they had received when she and Jon picked the girls up at their grandparents', she assumed they had been missed, too.

Although she couldn't see around the corner and down the hall, Beth heard the front door open and knew that Jon had just come inside. Since Saturday night and the kiss they shared, she had become very sensitive to his presence. And very hurt by his withdrawal from her.

Saturday night and the hayride had been wonderful. Beth knew she would never forget any part of it. Then Sunday morning brought a change in Jon.

Beth looked up as Jon stepped into the room. The girls saw him and squirmed away from her to run to him. Jon ignored her and scooped up both girls, one on each arm. His dimple flashed as he sat on the sofa to play with them, making them squeal and laugh.

Beth blinked away the tears that wanted to fall as she hugged her knees and watched them from the floor. Was it only last night when Jon had held her close in his arms? This morning his greeting might have come from a stranger. If she could just understand what had happened overnight. Where was the warm, gentle man she loved? Obviously, he regretted the kiss they shared as much as she treasured it.

For the next week, Beth's thoughts continued to bounce between the two extremes of Jon's behavior and brought her no comfort. She soaked up the sweet hugs and kisses from her daughters and enjoyed an occasional few moments of woman talk with Mary, but Jon's presence became a strain as he held her away with his polite aloofness.

Friday afternoon, Cecelia stopped by while the girls were napping. Beth took her into the family room where they could visit in comfort.

"Where's Robbie?" Beth sat in an overstuffed recliner as Cecelia took the sofa.

"At Mom's. I didn't want to be distracted, which is why I'm here during naptime."

"Oh, dear, this sounds serious." Beth tried to make her voice light.

"It is." Cecelia crossed her legs and relaxed against the back of the sofa. "It concerns my little brother and his next wife."

The air rushed from Beth's lungs as if Cecelia had punched her. "What are you talking about?"

"I'm talking about you and Jon. What is going on between you two?" She leaned forward, planting her elbow on her knee. "I saw him kiss you, Beth. The next morning, he treated you like you were a stranger, and now he's a bear at the office. What happened?"

Beth willed herself to not cry, even as a tear ran down her cheek. She swiped it away. "I guess you'll have to ask Jon, because I have no idea."

"I have asked him. He told me it's none of my business." Cecelia shook her finger at Beth. "And that tells me that something is wrong. What's he like here? Is he still treating you like an employee?"

A sound that could have been either laughter or a sob came from Beth's mouth as she tried to speak. "I've been wondering how to describe it—an employee that he doesn't much like would be even better."

Cecelia leaned back again and smiled. "Well, I guess that pretty much proves my theory. Jon is in love with you and he doesn't know what to do about it because he thinks all women are out to get something from him. Sharolyn wanted his money. You want his children."

"Yes, I want his children. But they are my children, too." A spark of anger rose in Beth's heart. "Doesn't he know that children need two parents? A mom and a dad both would be nice, don't you think?"

Cecelia laughed. "Maybe Jon doesn't know you are willing to share. It's up to you to convince him of that fact. You'll have to fight for his love, Beth. It may not be easy, but if you love him, it will be worth it."

The girls woke from their naps shortly after Cecelia left. Beth took them to the backyard to play, then Jon came home.

He lifted Lexie high into the air when Beth brought the girls inside to clean up for dinner. Stevie tugged on his pants leg. "Me, Dada, me."

He gave Lexie a kiss and set her down, then reached for Stevie. He held her high over his head and grinned at her. "So me wants attention, too, huh?"

He laughed and brought her down for a hug and kiss. Then he scooped Lexie up and headed for the dining room without so much as a word to Beth.

"Maybe I've become invisible and don't know it." Beth held her hand out and looked at it. Could invisible people see themselves? She rolled her eyes toward the ceiling and shook her head before following Jon and the girls. Invisibility might be the answer, but in order to become invisible to Jon for real, she would have to leave his house.

If it hadn't been for Mary and the girls, Beth would have left the table after five minutes. Never had she been so sick of politeness. If Jon directed even one sentence toward her during dinner without using "Please" and "Thank you" she decided she would jump up from the table and give him a hug. But he didn't.

After they ate, he stood and, without meeting her gaze, asked, "Would you please give both girls their baths tonight? I've got some briefs to look over before morning and could use the extra time."

Beth nodded. "Yes, that's fine, Mr. McDuff. I'll get right on it."

Jon's eyebrows rose at the use of his formal name. Beth turned away to unbuckle Lexie. She set her down, then took Stevie out of her highchair. Taking Lexie's hand and carrying Stevie, she left the dining room much slower than she would have liked as she felt Jon's gaze on her with every baby step Lexie took.

Later, in her bedroom, Beth lay across her bed and stared at the ceiling without seeing it. Something special happened on the night of the hayride. She had felt it and she knew Jon had, too. Why would he deny such a wonderful drawing together of their love? Cecelia was right. Jon loved her. She had felt his love surround her just as his arms had when they kissed. Tears trickled from the corners of her eyes into her hair, but she ignored them.

Yes, Jon loved her, but he would never acknowledge his love because he was afraid. She loved him so much she didn't know how she could continue living under the same roof with him. Yet, she could not move out because she could never give up either of her girls.

Before she went to sleep, Beth prayed that Jon's fears would soon be put to rest.

When morning came, Beth decided that if she couldn't leave Jon's house, she would do the next best thing. She would stay away from Jon as much as possible. Since he seemed to want her to be invisible, she would be.

So for the next week, Beth enlisted Mary to help her play a

game of Hide-and-Seek with Jon. When he entered a room, she found an excuse to leave. She continued eating dinner with him and Mary until Friday evening, when she carried three plates to the nursery and ate with the girls.

Half-expecting him to barge in on their picnic, her heart pounded every time she heard a sound outside the nursery. But he did not show up until the girls were in bed sleeping. Beth had just sat on the edge of her bed to pull her shoes off when she heard the knock at her hall door.

She stared wide-eyed at the door, knowing Jon waited on the other side. When he knocked again, this time louder, she decided she would have to answer before he woke the girls.

She pulled the door open. "Yes, Mr. McDuff. Did you want to see me?"

"Of course I want to see you." Jon pushed the door open farther. "Can we go someplace where we can talk? I don't want to wake the girls."

Beth shrugged while her heart beat an erratic staccato against her ribs. This was the showdown she had expected but dreaded. She walked around him and headed down the hall without a word.

Jon went to the family room and nodded toward the sofa. "Sit down, please."

There was that polite word again. Beth walked past the sofa to the overstuffed recliner she had sat in when Cecelia told her she would have to fight for Jon's love.

Jon frowned but sat on the sofa without comment. Then he looked at her. "Why weren't you at dinner tonight?"

"The girls and I had a picnic upstairs in the nursery."

"So you wouldn't have to eat with me."

Since he didn't ask a direct question, Beth didn't answer. She met his troubled gaze without waver.

"Don't think I haven't noticed that you've been avoiding

me, Beth. And why do you call me Mr. McDuff? I don't like it. What's going on?"

"Maybe you should tell me."

Jon leaned forward. "What do you mean by that? You're the one who walks out of the room every time I set foot in it. I haven't seen you except at dinner for over a week, and I scarcely see the girls, either. Are you trying to take them from me by turning them against me?"

"Of course not." Now Beth leaned forward. "I have never tried to take either girl away from you. Maybe at the very first that thought crossed my mind. But not now. Now that I know you."

"Then what else?"

Beth couldn't believe Jon had the nerve to confront her when he had been the one to pull away from her. She shook her head. "As if you don't know—" No, she would not play games with him. "You kissed me. Why did you do that, then ignore me ever since?"

Jon fell back against the sofa as if she had slapped him. He looked away from her toward the floor. "I haven't ignored you." He stood and moved toward the door as if he couldn't stand to stay in the same room with her. "There's no way I could ignore you, Beth."

Jon left Beth sitting in the recliner alone. She heard a door close and assumed he had gone into his den. She stood and went upstairs as a cold numbness settled around her heart.

She closed the door to her room and sat on her bed. A car door slammed outside and a motor started. Beth stepped across the room to look out the window and saw Jon's silver SUV back out of the driveway.

❧

Jon drove away from the house with moonlight bathing the hood of his SUV. He couldn't get Beth's question out of his mind. "Why did you kiss me?"

He parked in the deserted lot at the public park where he had taken Beth and the girls a couple of months ago. She had been beautiful then just as she was tonight. The difference being that she had been happy in the park playing with their little girls. Tonight, Beth was sad and hurt. And it was his fault.

Jon sat on the grassy bank beside the lake and watched moonbeams dance across the surface of the water. He thought of the night on the hayride when he held Beth close to his side. Kissing her had been the only option for him. When she'd looked up at him so trusting with the moon reflected in her eyes, he had reacted the only way he could.

When had he fallen in love with her? Jon picked up a small rock and skipped it across the water, sending the moonbeams into a dancing frenzy until they settled down again. How could he have fallen in love with her?

He had brought his daughter home where she belonged the only way he could, and that forced him to include Beth. But he hadn't intended to lose his heart to her.

He smiled. Beth loved him, too. He was sure of it. And Beth was nothing like Sharolyn. Beth wanted both babies in her legal custody just as much as he did. But, she would never try to take them from him. He knew that now. He lifted his eyes toward the star-studded sky as the wall of defense that Sharolyn had forced him to build around his heart suffered a lethal crack.

For the first time in years, Jon felt the moisture of tears fill his eyes, and he lowered his head in submission. Scenes from his past flashed through his mind as he gave them to the Lord in heartfelt prayer. One by one, the old hurts that Sharolyn had inflicted on him were brought before God and were healed. As he forgave Sharolyn, he also asked for forgiveness for his part in the pain of his past. As he bowed before God, he recommitted his life and his will to Him.

Much later, Jon wiped the tears away and blew his nose before he lifted his head with a smile. He realized that he no longer feared what loving Beth might do to him. He lay back on the grass and thought of Beth. Of the way she snuggled against him in the hay wagon. And he thought of the kiss they shared. Yes, Beth loved him just as much as he loved her. She loved God, too. He had seen the fruit of His spirit at work in her life. He need not fear being unequally yoked with Beth. They belonged together, brought together by God's will for their lives. Lexie and Stevie belonged to both of them.

Jon sat up, then sprang to his feet. He climbed the hill to his SUV with a light step. Tomorrow at the office would be the perfect time and place to begin his campaign to win Beth's hand in marriage. He could hardly wait to begin.

sixteen

Beth stayed up late watching for Jon's headlights but fell asleep without seeing them flash across her wall. She awoke the next morning to the raw facts of her life. Jon had walked out on her as if he couldn't stand to carry on a conversation with her any longer. He'd been gone a long time. She didn't know when he got home or if he had. But she knew he didn't love her.

She got out of bed and looked out the window. His silver SUV was parked in the driveway below. Beth sank back to the bed and buried her head in her hands. She couldn't go on living in the same house with him. She loved him too much. How could she continue to pretend that she didn't?

She thought of Lexie, and pain ripped through her heart. Her sweet little daughter. Although Beth had given birth to her, Lexie was not hers and never would be unless she decided to take the matter to court—a case which, even if she won, would put her at risk of losing Stevie. Maybe they could work out some sort of visitation without going to court. Beth knew that Jon didn't want the publicity that court would bring, and she didn't, either.

Stevie would be devastated to have to give up her new sister. Neither baby would understand the separation, but Beth knew as young as they were that they would adjust in time. Without doubt, giving up both Jon and Lexie would be the hardest thing she had ever done. But what else could she do?

She had her teaching certificate to fall back on. With her experience in day care, she should be able to find a preschool teaching position where Stevie could attend. With the money she had saved, she could get an apartment nearby so they could visit Lexie often.

Having decided her future, Beth dressed and checked on the girls in the nursery. Both still slept. She went to the closet and picked out matching outfits for them to wear. Their second birthdays were coming up in two weeks. She would wait until after their party to set her plan in motion.

Beth changed diapers and dressed the girls as they woke, then took them downstairs for breakfast. No more would she run from Jon. Surely she could carry on a business relationship with him for the next two weeks without further damaging her heart.

As she entered the kitchen, Jon stood from the table and took Lexie from Beth to put her in her highchair. Beth strapped Stevie in the other chair and noticed that Jon had just finished eating.

He gave Lexie a kiss on the forehead, then moved to do the same with Stevie. As he straightened, Beth had the irrational notion that he would kiss her next.

Instead he flashed her a quick smile. "I've got a ton of things to see to in the office today so I'm out of here. How is the birthday party coming for our soon-to-be two-year-olds?"

"Fine." Beth sat at the table. "Cecelia is coming later today to help me go over the details with the party planner. We are using clowns and a circus theme. The girls should love it."

"Yes, they should." Jon seemed distracted. "It sounds great. I'll see you later tonight. Actually, I may be later than usual. Have fun."

Beth watched him walk out without a backward glance and felt abandoned as she puzzled over his behavior. After the night before, she hadn't expected smiles and conversation from him. Except for the kiss that she still missed, he had been quite friendly.

As Mary bustled in from the kitchen with Beth's breakfast

of steaming pancakes to set in front of her, Beth forced her mind away from Jon. "Oh, you didn't need to do that. I could have gotten my own."

"It's no trouble." Mary smiled. "You do plenty around here taking care of our girls and helping me out every chance you get."

Beth shrugged. "Don't you think that's only fair considering you've agreed to watch the girls this afternoon while Cecelia and I go plan a party?"

Mary smoothed Lexie's hair and gave her a grandmotherly pat. "How hard can that be? They'll probably sleep most of the time you are gone."

Beth looked at Stevie, who held a bite of pancake in her hand trying to stuff it into her mouth. Then she looked at Lexie drinking from her sippy cup. In the months they had been together, the girls had grown so much. The food throwing and dropping of even four months ago had settled into a manageable mess on their trays. Lexie's vocabulary now equaled Stevie's. Or maybe her shyness had just disappeared, giving her the freedom she needed to talk.

Beth spent the morning playing with the girls. They enjoyed some time outdoors until the heat drove them inside. After a light lunch, Beth put the girls in their beds and left Mary in charge while she went downstairs to wait for Cecelia.

Dressed in jean shorts and a knit shirt, Cecelia looked very little like Beth's idea of a successful attorney. She looked down at her own slacks and shook her head. "For two cents, I'd go back upstairs and change into shorts, too, but I'm afraid I'll wake the girls if I do."

Cecelia shrugged. "I believe in comfort first. My appearance comes second."

Beth eyed the petite brunette and rolled her eyes upward. "You could wear anything and get by with it, and you know it. That's probably why you win all your cases. You are such a knockout in your attorney suits that no one pays attention to anyone else."

Cecelia laughed. "I don't know if that's a compliment or an insult. But I'm taking it as a compliment. Who cares about my wonderfully logical brain, which, of course, is the real reason I win all my cases?"

"Well, of course. Did I forget to mention that?"

The two women laughed and talked as Cecelia drove across town to a small shop snuggled into a strip mall not more than a couple of miles from Jon's house. The doorbell jingled as they went into the air-conditioned building. Shelves along the walls and freestanding racks held supplies for any type of party a person could imagine. Beth was glad they hadn't brought the children. A young girl behind the counter in back looked up and smiled. "Hi, what can I help you with?"

"We were hoping to finalize our plans for a party." Cecelia took the initiative and Beth gladly let her.

"Great!" Beth liked the enthusiasm of the clerk and hoped the clown for the party would be just as energetic. "What's the name on the party and when will it be?"

The girl pulled a file box forward and pulled a card from it as Cecelia gave her the information she needed. Beth was surprised that such a small business would have so many parties as the stuffed card file indicated. But Cecelia said they were good.

They went over the details of the party. Beth agreed to an air-filled slide and turned down the option of a pony ride. "I don't think so. The girls will be only two years old. Maybe when they are older."

A future party wouldn't happen unless she and Jon could come to some agreement concerning visitation. The thought of separating the girls and leaving Jon cast a cloud over the party planning for Beth.

When Cecelia and Beth returned to the car, Cecelia backed

out of the parking space and turned right onto the street. She drove for a short distance before pulling into a drive-in restaurant and stopping. "How about a cold drink?"

"Sounds good." Beth smiled her thanks.

While they waited for their soft drinks to be delivered, they talked about the upcoming party. "Are you happy with the way it's shaping up?" Cecelia asked.

Beth nodded. "Yes, I'm so glad you recommended the Party Place. They seem nice, and I'm sure they'll do a good job."

"Then what's wrong?" Cecelia's brown eyes grew as intense as Jon's did sometimes. "Is it Jon?"

"What do you mean? Nothing is wrong."

"Don't try to kid me, Beth. I've known you long enough now to know that something's eating away at you. How are things going with you and Jon?"

Beth tried to laugh, but her throat closed on the sound. She breathed in, trying to keep the hurt and confusion Jon's actions had caused her from showing on her face.

At that moment, the carhop carried their drinks to Cecelia's window, giving Beth the reprieve she needed. While Cecelia took the drinks and handed Beth hers, Beth prepared for the questions that she knew were coming. Jon's stubborn persistence had to have been inherited because Cecelia never let go when she thought she could help.

She paid the girl and turned to Beth. "Sorry. You were telling me about you and Jon."

Beth shook her head, almost amused at Cecelia's approach. "Actually, I couldn't have been, because there is no me and Jon."

Cecelia laughed. "Sure, and now you'll try to convince me I didn't see what I know I saw on the hayride."

When Beth didn't respond, she shrugged. "Okay, you don't have to tell me. Remember, I have a logical mind. I can figure out for myself that you and Jon have fallen in love and haven't the faintest idea how to deal with your feelings."

When Beth still didn't say anything, she shook her head. "That's funny, too, considering the fact that you've both been married before. I guess that proves that love is always new no matter how many times it happens to you."

"Please, Cecelia." Beth looked up from her soft drink. "I'll be honest with you. I love Jon very much, but that's where the love stops. Don't you think I'd know if he loved me?"

"What about the hayride? If that wasn't a man falling hard, I don't know what it was."

Beth took a sip before speaking. "I have no idea why he acted like he did on the hayride. I don't know why he has avoided me since. All I know is that I can't continue to live in the same house with him."

"Beth, no!" Cecelia laid her hand on Beth's arm. "Don't you dare leave. Please, just give him some time. You can't imagine the life he must have lived with Sharolyn. He loves you. I know he does. He's just having a hard time dealing with his feelings right now. Please, give him some time to work this all out."

Beth gave Cecelia a smile. "Don't worry. I haven't started packing yet. We have two weeks until the girls' birthdays. I won't do anything until after that."

Cecelia withdrew her hand. "Thank you. I'll pray that two weeks will be long enough. In the meantime, don't forget the McDuff family barbeque on the Fourth. Maybe being together with the family will help him see how much you mean to him."

Beth shrugged. "Don't count on anything, Cecelia. Jon has a mind of his own. If he can't love me, I don't want him. What hurts more than anything is Lexie. And Stevie. They are innocent, and no matter what I do, I'm going to hurt them both."

seventeen

Midmorning on the Fourth of July, Beth rode beside Jon in the front seat of his SUV over now familiar streets to his parents' house. He parked in front of the house and helped Beth with the girls.

She carried Lexie and the diaper bag, while Jon juggled Stevie and a large bowl of potato salad. Mary climbed from the back seat while she balanced a sheet cake.

Jon watched her until she got her footing, then grinned. "That cake is bigger than you are, Mrs. Garrett."

Faint color touched Mary's cheeks as she laughed. "Now, Mr. Jon, you know it isn't nice to stretch the truth."

He laughed with her, then fell into step with Beth. They followed the sidewalk around the house to the backyard, where they could hear voices and laughter. "Sounds like they are all here."

Beth smiled at him and nodded. Since the night he had blown up at her for avoiding him, he had been cheerful, almost as if he knew something that she didn't. He sought out her company, but their conversation never touched on anything personal. Yet in unguarded moments, Beth occasionally caught him looking at her as if he wanted to tell her something or maybe ask something. She didn't know what.

Now his smile hinted at more than surface friendliness. She tried to bury her love for him as she planned her escape, but as she looked into his eyes, she knew her efforts were useless. She loved Jonathan McDuff with or without Lexie and she always would.

"There are my sweet girls." Jon's mother lifted Lexie from

Beth's arms. His father took Stevie. Robbie bounced at their feet anxious to greet his cousins.

"Beth, over here," Cecelia called across the yard and waved a spatula.

Jon touched Beth's waist and gave a quick squeeze that set her pulse racing. "Go on and have fun. I want to see what my little brother is doing to that puppy—or dog. Looks like it has grown twice as much as our daughters have."

Beth watched him walk away and willed her heart to return to normal. What was the matter with him? Hugging her and talking as if they were a couple. Probably just a show for the family. If only it were true.

"Hi." Beth joined Cecelia and Donna at the grill. "What's going on? I thought outdoor cooking had been taken over by men."

The women laughed. Cecelia yelled toward the men, "Yeah, normally the men cook, but today we decided we wanted our food cooked so we could eat it."

"I heard that," her husband yelled back and they all laughed.

Beth helped Mary and Donna set out and arrange the food that had been brought. Beth put a stack of Styrofoam plates on the table along with some plastic service. She glanced toward Jon and saw that he now had the children and they were playing with Brad's puppy. Stevie hugged the dog, and Lexie squealed when it licked her sister. Jon laughed and grabbed both girls in a bear hug, taking them down on the grass with him, the puppy barking nonstop.

Beth's hands stilled as she watched the three people she loved most. Father and daughters. How she would love to capture the moment on film to take with her forever. But she had no camera, and soon there would be no more scenes such as this one to save.

Jon laughed and played with his daughters and Beth marveled at the freedom and happiness she saw on his face. In the months she had known him, she had never seen him so happy. Yet his happiness brought sadness to her heart because their time together could not last.

By evening the girls were exhausted and went to sleep on the way home. Jon and Beth carried them to the nursery and put them to bed. Jon paused at the door to look at them again.

Then he turned toward Beth. "Come downstairs with me for a glass of iced tea or some milk. Please? Mrs. Garrett won't mind looking in on the girls. She can hear them from her room."

Beth couldn't resist, knowing that such opportunities to spend time with Jon were few. She nodded and followed him out into the hall.

After letting Mary know where they would be, they went downstairs to the kitchen. A glass of iced tea sounded perfect to Beth. She stepped outdoors without hesitation when Jon suggested they sit on the patio to drink their tea.

Jon waited until Beth sat in one of the chairs, then he pulled another close and sat down. He smiled. "I had fun today. How about you?"

Beth nodded. "Your family is very nice. They all love the girls—both of them."

"That's because they are both our babies."

"You mean yours, don't you?"

Jon shook his head. "No, I mean ours. My family loves you, Beth."

Not liking the direction of their conversation, Beth said, "Brad and Donna think of their dogs as children, don't they?"

Jon smiled. "I think you are right. That will change now, though."

Beth's laughter sounded soft on the night air. "I guess so. I thought your mother was going to do handsprings when Brad made his announcement."

"My little brother a father." Jon shook his head. "I have a hard time imagining that."

Darkness settled around them as they sipped their tea and talked about nothing important. Beth felt Jon's presence stronger than ever as the seclusion of his backyard cut off the rest of the world. If only tonight could go on forever, she would be content.

Jon touched her hand and cupped her fingers beneath his. "It's getting late, Beth. I'm expecting some important papers to come in tomorrow at work and need my sleep. I'll walk you to your room."

Beth started to protest that she could find her way upstairs without his help, but kept her silence and stood. They set their empty glasses on the counter beside the sink and, with Jon's hand at her waist, walked toward the stairs.

Beth felt as if she were walking in a dream. Jon's presence and his solicitations confused her. If he didn't care for her, why did he continue to touch her? Was it pity? Did he know that she loved him and he felt sorry for her? She decided that the sooner she left, the sooner she could forget Jon, and the better that would be for everyone concerned. She didn't know how much more of this kind of behavior she could take from him, knowing that he didn't love her.

At the door to her room, he stopped and, catching her shoulders in his hands, turned her to face him. Beth's breath caught in her throat as she saw the intensity of his gaze when she looked up into his eyes. Then his gaze lowered seconds before he kissed her. The tender kiss lasted no more than a fleeting moment, yet would remain on her lips forever. Her mind had barely taken in his intentions before he turned and walked down the hall to the stairs and out of sight.

Beth pressed her fingers against her lips and stifled a cry. How could he be so cruel to give her one perfect day to remember and one perfect kiss to break her heart? She entered her room and closed the door while tears ran silently down her cheeks.

"I love you, Jon," she whispered into the silent room. "With all my heart, I love you. Why can't you love me, too?"

⁊⁊

Beth took the girls outdoors on the morning of their birthday and let them watch the party planners set up the inflatable slide that would be the highlight of their party. Similar to a giant slide used in carnivals and large gatherings, this smaller version topped out at only eight feet. Beth figured since the state day-care regulations considered six feet to be a safe height, eight would be plenty high enough for her rambunctious girls.

Stevie patted Beth's arm and pointed. "Pway, Mama. Lekkie and Teetee pway."

Beth picked her tiny daughter up and sat her on her lap. With very little encouragement, Stevie would be in the middle of the colorful blue, red, and yellow plastic that now covered their yard.

"Yes, we will play this afternoon. But we have to wait for the clown to come for your party."

"Pawty?" Stevie turned large brown eyes on her mother.

Beth smiled and hugged her before she made room for Lexie on her lap, as well. The little girl who had been so docile four months ago was now almost as inquisitive as Stevie. Beth didn't want either to get in the way of the workers.

Jon had left early that morning for what he said would be a quick trip into the office. Beth couldn't imagine what was so important that he had to work on the Saturday of his daughters' birthday party, but she figured it was none of her business. Besides, the party wouldn't be starting until after the girls had their naps.

"Mama." Lexie pointed as the compressor came on with a whirr and the colorful plastic began to move with the in-rush of air. "See, Mama."

"Yes, baby, I see." Beth relaxed as she knew the noise of the compressor would keep the girls on her lap. Together they watched the slide fill with air. Jon's large backyard seemed to shrink as the plastic shimmied and came alive, rising bit by bit to finally stand proud over the girl's play yard.

Their guests, both adults and children, should enjoy it. They had invited families from both churches who had babies in the nurseries with Lexie and Stevie as well as Jon's extended families, so several guests should be there. Beth had thought about inviting Bob, who had retained a distant friendship with her at church but decided that would not be such a good idea, considering Jon's reaction when Bob had come to the house.

"Time to go inside and eat now." Beth stood. "Then after a bath and nap, we should be ready for a party."

Stevie grabbed Lexie's hand and bent over to look into her face. Her eyes danced, and her dimple flashed as she said, "It's eat time, Lekkie. It's eat time."

Lexie laughed, and together the two girls went through the patio door ahead of Beth, holding hands and chanting in unison, "Eat time. Eat time."

Beth shook her head at them and smiled.

⁂

Three hours later, the backyard hummed with activity. Beth brought the girls, dressed in new, matching play rompers, outside through the patio door. With a tiny hand held in each of hers, she stopped just outside the door and stared at Jack and Irene Murdock, her mother and father.

"Mom and Dad!" Beth dropped her daughters' hands and stepped into the loving embrace of her own mother, then her father.

Jon stood just behind the Murdocks, a huge grin covering his face. Beth saw his self-satisfied expression and accused him as she stepped away from her father. "You didn't go to the office this morning. You went to the airport, didn't you?"

Jon laughed. "I've been busy."

As he spoke, a young woman stepped out from behind him.

"Lori!" Beth fell into her best friend's embrace. "I have missed you so much."

"No more than I've missed you." Lori looked over Beth's shoulder at the two little ones who stood watching the excitement with wide eyes. "Oh, no, she's grown so much I'm not even sure which is Stevie."

While Lori knelt in front of the girls, Beth caught Jon's gaze. "Thank you so much. It's not even my birthday."

When he just grinned, Beth looked back at her parents, who were eyeing their granddaughters with obvious pride.

Her mother looked from one baby to the other. "I can't get over how much alike they look. Who would have thought their coloring would be so similar? No wonder you didn't know. Who would?"

She knelt in front of the little girls and held her arms out. "How about it, Stevie? Does Grandma get a kiss?"

Stevie looked at her grandmother, then up at her grandfather. "Gam-maw." She grinned, letting her dimple flash. "Pam-paw."

In a second, Stevie burrowed into Gam-maw's arms, then Pam-paw took her while Beth introduced her mother and Lori to Lexie.

A tear found its way from the corner of Irene's eye. She brushed it away and smiled. "I'm sorry. I can't help but get weepy just thinking about how close we came to never seeing our baby. We'll find time to talk, dear, and you can tell me all about what's going on here. For now, I want to hold my grandbaby."

Lexie allowed her grandmother to hold her and, after a moment's hesitation, seemed to be content to stay with the Murdocks as they made over her and Stevie both. Beth allowed her parents to handle the girls as she kept Lori beside her and moved among the guests, welcoming each.

The clown was everything Beth had hoped for. She seemed to be everywhere encouraging the younger ones to participate and helping the little ones on the slide. With a pocket full of balloons and the ability to turn them into interesting animals, she kept the atmosphere jovial.

"Not a bad idea, huh?" Cecelia nudged Beth and pointed to the slide where Jon and Stevie sat at the top, ready to go down. Stevie's little hands clapped, and her smile lit her entire face.

Beth shook her head. "No, not a bad idea at all. The clown is good, too. I have to admit you do know your party planners. Everything seems to be going off without a hitch."

"Yes, well, I hope that trend continues." Cecelia moved on, and Beth didn't have time to wonder what she meant as one of the mothers from her church stepped into Cecelia's place.

"Beth, my kids are having a blast. They love that slide. Wherever did you get it?"

"Party Time Planners." Beth smiled. "The clown is one of their employees. She's good, isn't she?"

The mother nodded. "Very."

"Beth, when will you want the ice cream?" Mary asked. "I don't remember if you said before the gifts or after."

"Oh, dear." Beth stepped closer to Mary. "If we have the ice cream first, the girls will be too messy to touch the gifts. On the other hand, do you think they will leave their new toys and things to eat ice cream?"

Mary laughed. "Sounds like a real problem to me."

"Let's just go ahead with the ice cream first. I think that might be better."

"Fine. We'll get it set out here on the patio, and as soon as the girls blow out their candles, we'll start dipping." Mary bustled back into the house with a couple of teen girls she had recruited to help her.

Beth figured that was her cue to get Jon and the girls gathered up. She found Jon at the top of the slide again, except this time he had Lexie. She smiled, wondering who was having more fun, Jon or the girls. She waited at the base of the slide until they landed at her feet.

"Let's get Mama on the slide." Jon spoke to Lexie but grinned at Beth.

Beth laughed at the impish, little boy look in his eyes. "I will, I promise, but right now I need the girls on the patio so they can blow out their candles."

"Hey, hear that?" Jon hugged Lexie. "It's eat time."

"Eat time!" Lexie yelled, and Beth laughed along with Jon.

She met the amused glint in his eyes with one of her own. "You've been listening to the girls talk too much. Next thing we know you'll be in court talking like a two-year-old."

Jon threw back his head and laughed. "Who knows, maybe I'd win more cases if I did."

"More likely the judge would throw you out for confusing the English language."

Jon fell into step with Beth as she went in search of Stevie. They found her with her two sets of doting grandparents who, from all appearances, had become fast friends. Beth took her while Jon made the announcement that the candles were going to be blown out.

As their guests gathered, Jon and Beth stood with Lexie and Stevie behind the tables that held two large cakes. Both decorated with clowns in keeping with the circus theme, on one was written, HAPPY 2ND BIRTHDAY, LEXIE; on the other, HAPPY 2ND BIRTHDAY, STEVIE. Two candles occupied the center of each cake.

"Are we ready?" Jon looked at Beth for permission, then with encouragement, including a little help from their parents and cheering from their guests, both girls blew out their candles.

By the time the cake and ice cream had disappeared and the girls had opened their gifts, Beth wondered why she had ever agreed to have such a large party for them. But deep inside, she knew the answer to that. Sitting on a patio chair among a mountain of toys, videos, and clothes, Beth held Lexie close and fought the inevitable letdown. She had kept a happy face for Jon and the girls as well as for all of their guests.

Tomorrow she would have to face reality. Tomorrow she would make definite plans to leave Jon's house and his employment. She had put off as long as she could what had to be done. She loved Jonathan McDuff maybe even more than she had loved Steven. Maybe just in a different way. In any event, she knew that she loved him with all her heart.

But Jon didn't love her. And because he didn't, she and Stevie would have to go out on their own. She tried to convince herself that all would be better as soon as they got settled somewhere else, but her thoughts were as dark as the depression that hovered over her soul.

"What a stack of gifts for two little girls!" Cecelia took one from Jon and added it to the others. "Is that the last of them?"

Jon stood and handed Stevie to his sister. "No, actually there are two more gifts." He took Lexie from Beth and handed her to Cecelia. "See if you can find someone to help you with our birthday girls while I present the last two gifts to their mother."

Cecelia winked at Beth. "That won't be a problem."

Beth watched hands reaching for her girls as Cecelia walked away and wondered how much she knew about what Jon had in mind.

Then Jon slipped back into his chair by her side. With all their guests watching, he handed Beth two sheets of ivory parchment paper, rolled and tied with a ribbon.

When she looked at him, he said, "Please, will you read it? Aloud?"

Beth slipped the ribbon from the rolled paper and spread it out. At first glance the paper appeared to be some sort of legal document. At the top in bold letters she saw the McDuff Family Law letterhead. Below that in smaller letters were the words Attorneys-at-Law.

"Aloud, Beth." Jon spoke low. "Everyone would like to know what your gifts are."

Beth glanced up at friends and family who waited with expectancy on their faces. Lori gave her a smile, and Cecelia lifted one thumb while a wide grin covered her face. Beth picked up the document and began to read. "Consent for Adoption."

What? Her hands froze, but she did not outwardly react. In a normal sounding voice, she heard herself read as if the words came from someone else.

"Whereas the following findings of fact indicate that the welfare of the minor child, Alexis Gayle McDuff, so demands that adoption be approved in the Circuit Court of Jackson County, Missouri, Juvenile Division: 1. Said minor child was born on July 15, two years previous and Jonathan Ray McDuff, although not the child's biological father, has been in full and continual custody of said minor child to date. 2. The prior custodial mother of said minor child, Sharolyn Elaine McDuff, although not her biological mother, is now deceased."

Amid murmurs and whispers of disbelief from the gathered audience, Beth closed her eyes. What was going on? Jonathan had obviously devised some kind of legal ploy to take Lexie from her. She had known from the beginning that he would try to use the law to his advantage.

"There's more, Beth. Can you finish?" Jon's voice sounded gentle and caring. Beth knew better. This was the true Jonathan McDuff, attorney-at-law. All right, she'd read his Consent to Adopt, then she'd throw it in his face.

Straightening her back, she continued. "3. The minor child is suitable for adoption and the Petitioner, Jonathan Ray McDuff, is suitable as father of said minor child and has the ability to properly care for, maintain, and educate said minor child. 4. A full investigation, including DNA testing, has been made and proves without reasonable doubt that said minor child is the biological child of Elizabeth Anne Carter."

Beth's hands trembled as a collective gasp swept through the onlookers. She could sense them all scrambling to figure out the true nature of her relationship to Jon and the girls. So much for keeping their situation a secret. Now everyone would know their babies had been switched at birth. She ignored the space for her signature giving Jon the right to take her baby from her, and she flipped to the second page.

"Whereas the following findings of fact indicate that the welfare of the minor child, Stevie Elizabeth Carter, so demands that adoption be approved in the Circuit Court of Jackson County, Missouri, Juvenile Division: 1. Said minor child was born on July 15, two years previous and Elizabeth Anne Carter, although not the child's biological mother, has been in full and continual custody of said minor child to date. 2. The prior custodial father of said minor child, Steven W. Carter, although not the child's biological father, is now deceased."

Beth's eyes widened and her heart began to pound hard as she read the rest. "3. The minor child is suitable for adoption and the Petitioner, Elizabeth Anne Carter, is suitable as mother of said minor child and has the ability to properly care for, maintain, and educate said minor child. 4. A full investigation, including DNA testing, has been made and proves without reasonable doubt that said minor child is the biological child of Jonathan Ray McDuff."

While a ripple of voices rose around them, Beth managed to turn and look at Jon. She saw excitement in his eyes. And something else. Fear? Did he want her answer now? Her mind whirled in confusion. She couldn't stay near Jon now. How much worse it would be if she agreed to his crazy plan!

"Beth," Jon's voice penetrated the fog of her mind. "My second gift to you today is only yours if you accept it. I guess it really depends on how you look at what I'm offering."

As Beth took the second rolled parchment, her hand closed over something small and hard tied to the ribbon. At first she didn't know what it was—and neither did she care. As she slid the ribbon from the roll, the end of her finger slipped through the small hard circle. Afraid to see what she held in her hand, she closed her fingers around it and the ribbon and opened the paper.

"Please, will you read this one aloud, too?"

Beth looked into Jon's eyes and saw uncertainty. Why, if this document was so important to him, did he want her to read it before all these witnesses?

In bold letters under the letterhead were the words: PROPOSAL OF MARRIAGE. Beth skipped the heading and read, "Whereas Jonathan Ray McDuff has fallen completely and irrevocably in love with Elizabeth Anne Murdock Carter, he requests before the witness of family and friends that she consider his earnest proposal of marriage and agree to become his wife."

Her voice broke before she could finish the sentence in clarity. The remaining words swam before her eyes, and she let the document drop in her lap as she turned to the love of her life.

"Oh, Jon." She couldn't get anything else past the lump in her throat. Tears ran from her eyes as she laughed and threw her arms around his neck.

His arms were warm around her, holding her close. He whispered in her ear, "Does that mean yes?"

"Oh, yes, yes, it means yes." She squeezed him tight, then

someone started clapping and the others joined in. But Beth scarcely heard them as Jon caught her lips under his for a brief kiss that promised he would be hers forever.

He pulled away and grinned at her. "Where's the ring?"

"The ring?"

"Beth, the ring that was tied to the ribbon." Jon's grin disappeared. "Didn't you notice a ring?"

She smiled and brought her hand between them. She opened her fist and saw a gold and silver solitaire tied to a well-wrinkled ribbon. "Do you mean this ring?"

"Yes, I mean that ring." Jon took the ribbon and untied Beth's engagement ring. He slipped it on her finger, bringing an assortment of *oohs* and *aahs* from their audience. Just before a dozen admirers surrounded Beth, Jon managed to whisper that he would get a proper kiss later after their company left.

Beth smiled her promise, then reached for their two little girls as Cecelia and Lori placed them both on her lap. Jon slipped his arm around her shoulders, holding his family close.

A Letter To Our Readers

Dear Reader:

In order that we might better contribute to your reading enjoyment, we would appreciate your taking a few minutes to respond to the following questions. We welcome your comments and read each form and letter we receive. When completed, please return to the following:

Fiction Editor
Heartsong Presents
PO Box 719
Uhrichsville, Ohio 44683

1. Did you enjoy reading *This Child Is Mine* by Mildred Colvin?
   ❑ Very much! I would like to see more books by this author!
   ❑ Moderately. I would have enjoyed it more if

   _____
   _____
   _____

2. Are you a member of **Heartsong Presents**? ❑ Yes ❑ No
   If no, where did you purchase this book? _____
   _____

3. How would you rate, on a scale from 1 (poor) to 5 (superior), the cover design? _____

4. On a scale from 1 (poor) to 10 (superior), please rate the following elements.

   ____ Heroine   ____ Plot
   ____ Hero   ____ Inspirational theme
   ____ Setting   ____ Secondary characters

5. These characters were special because?_____
_____
_____

6. How has this book inspired your life?_____
_____
_____

7. What settings would you like to see covered in future
   Heartsong Presents books? _____
_____
_____

8. What are some inspirational themes you would like to see
   treated in future books? _____
_____
_____

9. Would you be interested in reading other **Heartsong
   Presents** titles? ❏ Yes ❏ No

10. Please check your age range:
       ❏ Under 18   ❏ 18-24
       ❏ 25-34   ❏ 35-45
       ❏ 46-55   ❏ Over 55

Name_____
Occupation _____
Address _____
City_____ State_____ Zip_____

SAN FRANCISCO

4 stories in 1

Four independent women in the San Francisco bay area are about to be swept into a wave of romance. Letting go to romance will take each woman a step of new faith. Will the arms of love catch them—or will they be shattered by a dream?

Four complete inspirational romance stories by author Kristin Billerbeck.

Contemporary, paperback, 464 pages, 5 ³/₁₆" x 8"

Presents

Great Inspirational Romance at a Great Price!

Heartsong Presents books are inspirational romances in contemporary and historical settings, designed to give you an enjoyable, spirit-lifting reading experience. You can choose wonderfully written titles from some of today's best authors like Hannah Alexander, Andrea Boeshaar, Yvonne Lehman, Tracie Peterson, and many others.

When ordering quantities less than twelve, above titles are $2.97 each.
Not all titles may be available at time of order.

HEARTSONG
PRESENTS

If you love Christian romance…

$10.99

You'll love Heartsong Presents' inspiring and faith-filled romances by today's very best Christian authors…DiAnn Mills, Wanda E. Brunstetter, and Yvonne Lehman, to mention a few!

When you join Heartsong Presents, you'll enjoy 4 brand-new mass market, 176–page books—two contemporary and two historical—that will build you up in your faith when you discover God's role in every relationship you read about!

Mass Market 176 Pages

Imagine…four new romances every four weeks—with men and women like you who long to meet the one God has chosen as the love of their lives…all for the low price of $10.99 postpaid.

To join, simply visit www.heartsong presents.com or complete the coupon below and mail it to the address provided.

✂ -

YES! Sign me up for Heartsong!